MEN *in* **UNIFORM**

Courteous, courageous and commanding—
these heroes lay it all on the line for the
people they love in more than fifty stories about
loyalty, bravery and romance.
Don't miss a single one!

VICTORIA PADE

ON PINS AND NEEDLES

Published by Silhouette Books

America's Publisher of Contemporary Romance

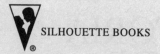 SILHOUETTE BOOKS

Recycling programs
for this product may
not exist in your area.

ISBN-13: 978-0-373-36294-3

ON PINS AND NEEDLES

VICTORIA PADE

is a *USA TODAY* bestselling author of numerous romance novels. She has two beautiful and talented daughters—Cori and Erin—and is a native of Colorado, where she lives and writes. A devoted chocolate lover, she's in search of the perfect chocolate chip cookie recipe. For information about her latest and upcoming releases, and to find recipes for some of the decadent desserts her characters enjoy, log on to www.vikkipade.com.

To Jill Megan Morian, acupuncturist extraordinaire.

Chapter 1

MEGAN BAILEY DOUBLE-CHECKED her treatment room
to make sure everything was ready. Her muscle testing vials were in order and all accounted for. The Soft
Sounds Of Nature CD was in the CD player. There was
a crisp sheet over her treatment table and she fluffed
the pillow at the head of it just for good measure. Her
needles were in the drawer of the corner cupboard where
cotton balls and alcohol were also amply stocked. The
dimmer on the light switch was working.

She was all set. All set for her first client in her new
office. Hopefully the first of many.

Not that she was expecting a sudden surge of business, because she wasn't. She was realistic. She knew
she was only breaking the ice in the small town and
that it would take a while to build any kind of practice
here.

After all, Elk Creek, Wyoming, was about as old-
fashioned, traditional, and conservative a small town
as anyone could find anywhere. Which probably didn't
make it the wisest choice for a place to open an office for

Megan to practice acupuncture and her sister Annissa to do massage therapy.

But Elk Creek was the site of the sole piece of property that the Bailey family owned—the twenty acres on which sat the old farmhouse Megan's and Annissa's maternal grandfather had built. It was also the place Megan and Annissa had lived for the longest amount of time—from birth until Megan was twelve and Annissa was eleven.

That made it seem like home. Like the place to come to when she and Annissa decided they wanted to finally put down roots.

So that's what they'd done. They'd moved back to Elk Creek, into the old farmhouse that was costing them a fortune to get into livable condition, and they'd set up shop in this storefront on Center Street.

But the office had been open for two weeks now and so far Annissa hadn't had a single call for her services as a massage therapist and herbalist, and Megan's days had been filled only with putting up posters and a single meeting with the town doctor to introduce herself, lay out her credentials and talk about the uses and success rates of acupuncture and how it might be applied in conjunction with Western medicine or when Western medicine failed. Particularly her specialty—allergy elimination acupuncture.

We knew it wouldn't be easy, she reminded herself as she checked the clock on the wall and realized she had less than fifteen minutes until her appointment.

She and Annissa realized that introducing non-traditional forms of health care was bound to meet some resistance. But after being raised by two eternal hippie-flower children, neither Megan nor Nissa were unfamiliar with being considered out-of-the-norm weirdos and they were determined to make a go of it here no matter what.

And today could be the start of that, Megan thought. The start of establishing themselves in their old hometown. Especially since Megan's appointment was with Josh Brimley.

She had only the vaguest memory of who he was. All she really recalled was that the Brimley family lived on a small ranch down the road from her family's place and that there had been a lot of them. Six brothers, if she wasn't mistaken.

She wasn't sure in what order they came but she did know that Josh had not been in her grade in elementary school or in Nissa's class one year behind hers. Nissa had known a Devon Brimley and Megan thought it was Scott Brimley who had been her age, but beyond that neither of them was sure where in the pecking order Josh Brimley fell. Or anything about him. Except that he was now Elk Creek's sheriff.

Their paths hadn't crossed in the three weeks Megan and Annissa had been in town but they were hoping that the very fact that he was the sheriff would carry some weight. Getting a man who held a respected public position to come in for acupuncture seemed like a good way to get word out that she and Nissa could provide valid services to the community.

At least that was what they were counting on and why Megan felt as if there was a lot riding on this single appointment, and why she'd accepted it for five o'clock on a Saturday afternoon.

When she was satisfied that she was prepared for her client, she left the treatment room and went into the bathroom to check her appearance. She wanted to make a good first impression so she'd opted for a loose cotton jumper that went nearly to her ankles and covered the white crewnecked T-shirt she wore underneath it. She also had on her best clogs and her lucky bracelets—ten thin copper bracelets she wore on her left wrist.

A quick check in the mirror told her she looked all right but still she ran a brush through her hair until the pale-blond straight strands lay smoothly all the way to the blunt-cut ends that fell about six inches below her shoulders.

She didn't wear makeup but she had used a henna mascara to darken her eyelashes so her blue eyes didn't seem too washed out and she decided it didn't need any freshening. She was also grateful that her skin had always been good—something she attributed to a healthy diet—and that her cheeks had a natural rosiness to them. It helped boost her confidence to see that she appeared fresh-faced even though she hadn't really done anything since early that morning.

She did apply an organic moisturizing lip balm to add some gloss to her lips, and she blotted a bit of shine from her thin, straight nose before she judged herself presentable and went out to the desk she and Annissa shared in the waiting room of the office.

Not that they were sharing it at that exact moment. Nissa was doing free chair massages at a Ladies' League meeting and potluck dinner—again in an effort to spark some interest in their services.

Two huge windows made up the waiting room's front wall, leaving it exposed to the street and the street exposed to Megan as she sat behind her desk to gather together the packet of papers she would give the sheriff on his way out after their initial appointment. There were two articles—one explaining acupuncture in general and the other outlining the merits of allergy elimination acupuncture. There was also a brief biography that listed her education and experience, a pay schedule, and another sheet that touted Annissa's services, along with coupons for a ten-percent discount on either an acupuncture treatment or a massage.

Megan tapped all the pages into line, added one of her cards and one of Annissa's to the top left hand corner and stapled the whole packet together just as a rotund man who looked about her age paused outside.

She smiled at him through the window and he inclined his head, clad in a cowboy hat.

Was he Josh Brimley?

There wasn't a badge of any kind in sight and he wasn't wearing a uniform. At least not an officer-of-the-law uniform. Instead the man had on what seemed to be the uniform of Elk Creek—cowboy hat and boots, blue jeans and a Western shirt.

But that didn't mean he *wasn't* the sheriff. And since he was lingering outside the door, Megan thought it was possible he might indeed be Josh Brimley. And that maybe he was having second thoughts. That maybe he wouldn't come in at all without some encouragement.

But if that was the case, she wasn't going to let him get away. So she got up and went to the door, opening it to smile again at the man with the hooked nose and the very small eyes as he took a flyer out of the basket she and Annissa had set out when they'd opened for business two weeks ago.

"Hi," she greeted him warmly.

"'Lo," came the gruff reply.

She held out her hand. "I'm Megan Bailey."

The man looked from her outstretched hand to her face and back to her hand again before he accepted it. But he didn't offer his name.

So Megan said, "You wouldn't happen to be Josh Brimley, would you?"

The man gave her a look that said it was a dumb question. "No, I wouldn't be. Name's Burns," he finally informed her.

"Ah. Well, I'm happy to meet you, Mr. Burns. Can I help you with anything or answer any questions you might have?"

"Wife's curious about this hooey. Wanted me to bring 'er home somethin' about it."

Not a warm welcome or a hearty endorsement but Megan didn't let it daunt her.

"You lookin' fer the sheriff?" the man asked then. "'Cuz he's down on the corner there, keepin' an eye on this place."

Mr. Burns's tone was suspicious but it was the news that Josh Brimley was standing off in the distance, watching the office as if he were on a stakeout that really dismayed Megan. It didn't seem like a good sign.

She glanced in the direction Mr. Burns had indicated with a pointing of his nearly nonexistent chin and discovered that there was, indeed, another man three doors down, leaning a shoulder against one of the many Victorian lampposts that lined either side of Center Street, his hands in the pockets of a pair of tight blue jeans, one ankle crossed over the other.

But before she could decide how she should handle what appeared to be the sheriff's reluctance to come any closer, Mr. Burns piped up in a louder voice and called, "Lady's askin' after ya, Josh."

That news did not seem to please the other man.

In fact, even though his face was mostly lost in the shadow cast by the brim of his own cowboy hat, his jaw seemed to clench.

An even worse sign.

"That so?" he called back as if he didn't have the foggiest idea why Megan might be inquiring about him.

That was when it occurred to her that he might have been waiting to come in for his appointment until the disparaging Mr. Burns moved on so that no one would see him.

So much for hopes of word getting around and having a man who held a respected public position as a client breaking the ice around here and helping to get her started. At that point, Mrs. Burns's curiosity seemed more promising.

But as Megan stood there she thought that she had two choices. She could say something that would give Josh Brimley away and get the word out herself that he had an appointment with her, or she could respect what seemed to be his desire not to have that known and just hope that when her treatments were successful, he'd admit to having had them.

She opted for the second scenario and in a voice loud enough for him to hear, she said, "I was just hoping to have the sheriff check our locks for us at some point, for safety's sake." Then, only to Mr. Burns, she added, "I hope your wife will come in and see us."

And with that, Megan turned on her heels and returned to her office, keeping her fingers crossed that Mr. Burns would finally be on his way and Josh Brimley would feel free to keep his appointment under the auspices of giving his stamp of approval to her office security.

Although she was beginning to worry that he might not keep the appointment at all. That he might just go the other way and be a no-show.

But her fears were unfounded. After Mr. Burns had disappeared in the opposite direction and the coast was presumably clear, in came Josh Brimley.

Megan was nonchalantly watering the fern in the corner of the waiting room when he did and it struck her almost instantly that even though the space was large, the sheriff seemed to fill it.

He was a big man, she realized as she set the watering can down and turned to face him. He was probably three inches over six feet tall, with shoulders so broad it was a wonder they'd fit through the door. He wore a pale-gray Western shirt tucked into his jeans and there didn't seem to be an ounce of fat on him. Instead he was a tower of lean muscle in long legs, narrow hips and a waist that V'd sharply up to those massive shoulders.

But it wasn't sheer size that was responsible for his command of the room. He had a kind of intangible presence that she thought would cause the phenomenon no matter what room he entered.

Then he took off his hat and Megan's gaze went naturally to his face.

He was no pretty boy but he had rugged good looks in a face of perfect sharp angles and planes. Perfect enough to cause a little catch in Megan's breathing as she took it all in.

His brow was square, his nose was straight, and his lips had an intriguing suppleness to them that made her want to see them slide into a smile. His well-defined jawline was shaded by the hint of a thick beard, and to top it all off, he had the most incredible midnight-blue eyes she'd ever seen.

With his hat in one large, adept hand he ran the other over the short bristles of hair the color of antique oak, leaving it slightly spiky on top before he leveled those amazing eyes on her.

And the oddest thing happened. Megan felt a buzzing intensity ripple through her almost as if he'd actually touched her.

Of course she ignored it, held out her hand the same way she had to Mr. Burns, and said, "In case you didn't know, I'm Megan Bailey."

But unlike Mr. Burns, Josh Brimley didn't take his eyes off her face even as he accepted her hand.

"Josh Brimley," he said unnecessarily in a voice as deep and rich as aged bourbon.

His hand was strong, callused and warm to the touch, and having it wrapped around hers did wild and wicked things to the pit of her stomach. But she ignored that, too, clearing her throat so that when she spoke again her own voice didn't ring with the effects he was having on her.

"I don't remember too many people from around here so I assume not too many of them remember me, either," she explained. "I just thought it wouldn't hurt to introduce myself."

"My brother Scott remembers you and your sister from grade school, but I'm two years older than he is and I can't say that I have much recollection of the two of you. I know your place, though. I was amazed to see anyone trying to live in it again. It's gotten pretty rundown over the years."

"Worse than we expected," she confirmed. "When we decided to come back we thought the house would need a little paint, a little fixing up. But so far it's needed a whole lot more than that. Today we're having to put in a new septic tank. When we left this morning there was so much machinery in our backyard it looked like a construction site."

"I can imagine," he said, smiling just enough to cut creases down both cheeks and prove just how lithe those lips were. It also increased the level of his handsomeness by another notch. If that were possible.

Megan gave herself a quick, silent talking-to about the inadvisability of letting herself be distracted by a client's appearance and cut the chitchat to get down to business before she completely forgot herself and why he was here.

"When your secretary made the appointment—at least I assumed it was your secretary—"

"Millie. She's the dispatcher and the postmistress, too," he explained.

"Oh. Well, she said you're suffering from an allergy that Dr. McDermot thought might benefit from acupuncture."

"Mmm," he answered noncommittally, glancing around at the waiting room. "And I'll take a look at your locks, if you want, too."

Megan had almost forgotten she'd said that only moments before outside. But now that he'd brought it up, she said, "I'm not really worried about the locks. It just seemed as if you might not be comfortable letting Mr. Burns know you were scheduled to come in for acupuncture so I thought I'd cover your tracks."

The sheriff's full eyebrows drew together at that. "I wasn't worrying about who knew or what anybody thought. I just wasn't sure I was going to actually do this," he answered matter-of-factly. "No offense, but it just seems like some kind of hocus-pocus or voodoo or something. Not anything that could actually do me any good."

"Ah, I see. I appreciate your honesty," she said, not taking offense because it was a sentiment she'd been confronted with before. "But if Dr. McDermot recommended me he must have told you that acupuncture can be effective."

"He wasn't all that convinced himself. But this damn—this allergy thing has just come up recently and the medicines he's given me make me fuzzy-headed and too tired to think. I can't have that on this job. So Bax thought I might as well give you a try."

She couldn't be sure but she thought there might be a bit of innuendo to the last part of that statement. Especially since the *give you a try* had come with the tiniest upward quirk to one side of his mouth. But once more she opted for pushing aside the idea and sticking to matters at hand.

"In other words, I'm the last resort," Megan concluded.

"That's about it."

"And you think you're wasting your time," she finished what he seemed to have left unsaid. "That's okay. You aren't the first person I've had to prove myself to and I'm sure you won't be the last."

His very attractive mouth eased into another smile, as if he thought he'd gotten her goat and it pleased him.

Well, he hadn't gotten her goat. And to show him, she put some effort into sounding more professional.

"Have you had allergy tests to isolate what you are and what you aren't allergic to?" she asked.

"No, but I can pretty much tell. Horses and hay seem to trigger it. And since, besides being sheriff and being around them pretty much everywhere I go, I need to work the family ranch, I have to do something about it."

"Which is why you're here."

He merely inclined his head to concede the point.

"I'll need to do some testing of my own—" Megan held up her hand when he opened his mouth to protest. "Unlike what an allergy doctor would do, my way of testing is much easier and absolutely non-invasive. It's simple muscle testing through applied kinesiology."

"Whatever that is."

"You'll see as soon as we get started. But I need to isolate everything you're allergic to. For instance, if you were allergic to bacon you might have a sensitivity to pork, or it might be the nitrates the meat is cured with that bother you. I'd have to know which it is before you could actually be cleared."

"For takeoff?"

Okay, so he could make her smile and she liked that in a man, too. She still tried to maintain her perspective, though, by reminding herself that he thought she was a quack. "No, not cleared for takeoff. Cleared of the allergy. That's what it's called when I cure you," she said with exaggerated bravado.

He caught it. "When you *cure* me. Do you do laying on of hands and faith healing, too?"

"No, just acupuncture." And she was enjoying their back-and-forth teasing too much, so she amended her tone to a more authoritative one and said, "Shall we get started?"

But before he could answer, the front door opened suddenly to admit the contractor Megan had hired to replace her septic tank.

It surprised both Megan and Josh. Their focus on each other had been so intense that neither of them had seen him coming despite the fact that anything was hard to miss through the huge windows.

"Never thought I'd find you both in one place," Burt Connors said by way of greeting. "Glad to see it, though. Saves me a trip."

"Hi, Burt," the sheriff answered as if they were old friends.

"Josh," the excavator countered the same way.

"What's up?"

Apparently Josh Brimley thought he should take over. But since Megan was still trying to figure out why her contractor had been looking for her *and* the sheriff, she guessed it was just as well.

"Got that old septic tank out and put in the new one," Burt Connors informed them both. "But when we were coverin' it up again we dug a little in another spot for fill dirt and found somethin' else. Somethin' that looks like sheriff business."

"You found *sheriff business* in my backyard?" Megan said.

"Yes, ma'am. Looks like a skeleton. A human skeleton."

"Are you sure it isn't just an old family grave?" Josh asked reasonably.

"Sure enough. He's not too deep, there's no coffin and it looks like the guy was planted belongings and all. I think you better come take yourself a gander, Josh. And you, too, Ms. Bailey. This ain't no kind of formal buryin'. I'm bettin' we've opened up somethin' somebody thought would never come to light."

Josh Brimley turned those dark, dark blue eyes to

Megan again, this time from beneath one raised brow. "Anything you'd like to tell me?"

"Only that I don't have the foggiest idea what's going on."

But he didn't look completely convinced of that as he led the way out of her office.

Chapter 2

THE OCCASIONAL CAR ACCIDENT. Reckless driving. Speeding. Mailbox bashing. Minor vandalism. Cattle tipping. Drunk and disorderly conduct. Brawling. A break-in here and there—in the history of Elk Creek that was as bad as it got in the way of crime. Until now.

It was a little hard for Josh to believe that only three months into his run as sheriff he was looking at what seemed to be a murder. But it didn't take him long after reaching the Bailey place and looking over what had been unearthed to realize that could well be just what he was confronted with.

"I've put up the crime scene tape to cordon off the area. Your men can work around it," he told Burt Connors when he had the burial site contained.

Chaos reined supreme in the Bailey backyard since Burt insisted that he and his crew had to finish up their work so the Bailey sisters would have use of their plumbing facilities by nightfall. And although Josh was fairly certain curiosity in what that same crew had uncovered was the real reason behind their lingering, he didn't object. He had work of his own to do as he used a whisk

broom to carefully and methodically brush away the soil
that remained partially obliterating the skeleton so that
the entire grave and its contents were visible.

Josh had trained with the Wyoming sheriff's department and he knew all the procedures, including those
for a crime of this magnitude. He knew the procedures
by heart. But a murder investigation was the last thing
he'd ever expected to actually have to do in his small
hometown.

Of course he should have known better than anyone
that not many things turned out the way a person expected them to. But still, it was a sobering job that lay
ahead of him.

Daylight had disappeared by the time Josh backed
away from the freshly cleared hole, confident that he'd
done all he should do on his own for the moment. But
he did avail himself of Burt Connors's offer of floodlights to illuminate the area and then hunkered down
on his heels at the graveside to get a closer look at what
he'd actually exposed while he waited for the sheriff's
department's forensic team.

Along with the bones that had been discovered, there
was a knapsack and the clothes the victim had worn.
The clothes were nondescript, the same kind of clothes
he and most everyone else around these parts wore—a
plain shirt, blue jeans, cowboy boots.

The sole of one of the cowboy boots was down to
its last layer of leather and the fact that there was a tear
in one knee of the jeans and the shirt was threadbare
around the edges led him to believe this hadn't been a
prosperous man. Josh was betting that when they got

into the knapsack that rested alongside the skeleton, they'd find all his worldly goods contained in it.

The knapsack itself was a well-worn canvas bag and, although Josh was careful not to disturb anything so that the scene would be intact for the forensics unit, there was a local newspaper sticking out far enough for him to read the date without touching anything. It was a June newspaper. Eighteen years old.

After his arrival on the scene and his initial look into the grave Josh had radioed Millie Christopher—the woman Megan Bailey had referred to as his secretary—and had Millie look for any missing persons reports that might be on file at the office.

Millie said she'd look, but she knew for a fact that in the entirety of her thirty-eight years as the sheriff's girl-Friday, the only missing persons case there had ever been was a teenage girl who had turned out to be a runaway in 1982.

So much for hoping for an easy lead.

The forensics unit arrived then and Josh met them at their van, introducing himself and filling them in as he took them to the site. Once they got to work he was left to stand by and oversee their first few chores—taking pictures of the scene from all angles, and closely observing and describing in notes the placement of everything. Nothing could be moved until that was accomplished.

Within moments of the arrival of the forensics unit, two state patrol cars showed up, too. The officers had heard over their radios what was going on and had come to see if they could help. They couldn't, but they stayed around anyway, adding to the number of onlookers. One of whom, of course, was Megan Bailey.

Her sister hadn't returned yet but Megan had set up a card table with beverages and bran muffins for anyone who might want them.

Josh was tempted to shout over to her "What do you think this is? A tea party?"

But he refrained. It wasn't as if she appeared to be enjoying this because she didn't. On a rational level, Josh knew she was only being considerate of everyone's comfort. But still, just having her there—even out of the way beside her back door—was damn distracting.

At least it was damn distracting to him.

No one else seemed to pay her much mind beyond quick trips to the table to accept her hospitality before getting right back to work. But for Josh it was a different story.

Here he was, in the middle of something as big as a potential homicide and his thoughts—and eyes—kept wandering to Megan Bailey.

She's a flake, he told himself impatiently. Allergy elimination acupuncture—that was how she made her living, for crying out loud. With a gazillion bracelets on one wrist and those nutty-looking wooden clogs on her feet instead of regular shoes. A flake. That's what she was all right.

It didn't matter if she had gleaming blond hair that was so silky and flawless that even the floodlights made it seem to glow. It didn't matter that she had skin like porcelain or high cheekbones the color of summer roses. It didn't matter that she had a small, sculpted nose or lips that gave off the sensuality of a siren. It didn't matter that she had a perfect, compact little body with just enough up front to make a man wonder. And it sure as hell didn't matter that she had long-lashed doe-eyes the pale color of cream stained by blueberries.

The only thing that mattered was that she was a flake. A flake with a body buried in her backyard.

And even if she hadn't had a body in her backyard, she was *not* the kind of woman he should be distracted by.

He'd learned his lesson the hard way. Taught in painful detail by an off-the-wall woman. He definitely didn't want anything to do with another one.

Plain, down-to-earth females—those were the only kind he intended to give a second look, and Megan Bailey was a long way from that.

So why was he standing there, watching her open a soda can for the lead forensic investigator and noticing how delicate her hands were? Why was he straining for a look at her shape through the gossamer draping of her dress when he should be straining for a look at his crime scene? Why was he memorizing the way her hair fell around her shoulders rather than memorizing every word that passed from one forensic investigator to the other? And why on God's green earth was he paying more attention to a detail like her earlobe and the sweet spot just below it than to the details of his own job?

He didn't know why. He only knew that even though he felt as if he was being derelict in his duties, he still couldn't tear his eyes off her….

"I think we can start to move 'im out, see if there's

anything important underneath 'im, and get everything to the lab now."

The head of the forensic team's voice yanked Josh's attention away from Megan and his confused reveries, and back to what he was supposed to be concentrating on.

"Anything you can tell me yet?" he asked.

"Not much. So far there's no obvious indication of cause of death—like a bashed-in skull. But these are hardly optimum working conditions. Hopefully we'll be able to tell more at the lab and won't need a forensic anthropologist. There are only a handful of those in the whole country. For now the best I can do is put the time of death at June, eighteen years ago."

"Yeah, I saw the date on the newspaper, too."

The team leader shrugged. "You probably already guessed it's the skeleton of a man, too, from the clothes. I'd say he was in his midfifties. Probably Caucasian. Not well-off. We haven't gotten into the knapsack yet, could be something in there will tell us more."

Josh nodded. "Just let me know as soon as you find anything out."

"Your case. You'll be the first."

The septic tank crew seemed to have finished up, too, because they were clearing out as Burt Connors stood talking to Megan Bailey at the card table. Josh crossed to them and drew both glances.

"Find anything out?" Burt asked without preamble.

"Not yet. But I'm going to need a few preliminary questions answered," Josh said, aiming the statement at Megan.

"Can we do it inside? It's getting kind of chilly out here," she responded, crossing her arms over her middle to rub them with those long-fingered hands he'd been watching before.

Something caught in Josh's throat at the sight, and what he really wanted to do was put his arms around her and warm her up himself….

He nixed that idea in a hurry, wondering where the hell it had come from in the first place.

Then he said, "Yeah, no matter how nice the days are this time of year, April nights cool off plenty. If you can't take it, go ahead in. I'll be there as soon as everybody out here is gone."

Megan's eyebrows rose slightly at the gruffness in his tone but he couldn't worry about that. She didn't have to like him. He didn't *want* her to like him. As far as he was concerned she was part of a murder investigation and that was it.

Josh turned back to the excavation site then. And as he retraced his steps he told himself to use this time before he went in to question Megan Bailey to get a handle on whatever this was that was going on with him.

She's a flake, he repeated to himself as a reminder of why he had no business noticing the things he'd been noticing about her, or thinking the things he'd been thinking about her. Why he should know better than to notice those things or think those things.

But neither the fact that he considered her a flake nor the fact that she might be involved in some way with a murder, kept him from wishing the state patrolmen, Burt

Connors's crew, and the forensics team would hurry up and clear out of there.

Because the sooner they did, the sooner he could get back to Megan Bailey.

And be alone with her again....

Megan sat in her kitchen, trying to sort through what had happened today.

There was no denying that returning to Elk Creek had been fraught with complications. The house had been in such disrepair. Worse than room after room of cobwebs, four broken windows, and a need for new paint inside and out, there had been problems with the electrical wiring, old appliances that had refused to come out of retirement, and the need for a whole new septic system.

Not only had she and Nissa had to do all the home repairs they could possibly do themselves, they'd also had to set up their office on top of it—complete with more cleaning and painting and furniture moving—because they hadn't been able to afford to hire help.

Certainly clients hadn't been clamoring to their door and they hadn't been met with a warm reception.

And now this.

Someone was buried in the backyard? Megan didn't know what to make of *that*. Especially when Josh Brimley turned officious and contrary on her. As if she'd had something to do with it.

Did he think she and her sister had brought the skeleton with them and planted it behind the house for fun? Or maybe he thought it was part of some *hocus-pocus* or *voodoo* ritual since that's what he considered the practice of acupuncture.

Well, fine. It was good to know from the start what kind of man he was. That he was *not* the kind of man she would ever allow to get close to her again. The next man she let into her life was going to be accepting and tolerant and receptive. He was going to be open-minded, liberal, enlightened and unbiased.

In short, he wasn't going to be anything like Noel.

And so far, Josh Brimley seemed a whole lot more like Noel than not.

Hocus-pocus and voodoo, Megan thought, taking offense now to what she hadn't taken offense to when he'd said it earlier. And that facetious, *if you can't take it...*

As if she should stay standing out in the chilly night air as punishment. As if, under the circumstances, she didn't *deserve* to come in out of the cold.

He might be incredible to look at, but now she knew what was under the surface—he wasn't just a skeptic who could be won over to the idea that there were viable alternatives in the world, to the fact that not everyone had to be a carbon copy of everyone else. He wasn't a person who could learn to appreciate diversity. He was judgmental, close-minded, and suspicious. Suspicious of *her,* of all things.

Megan had worked up quite a head of steam by the time the knock came on the back door just then.

"Yes," she called in a clipped tone that lacked all welcome.

And when Josh Brimley opened the door and stepped

inside, she didn't stand to greet him and she absolutely refused to offer him something to drink to warm up—like a cup of the spice tea she'd fixed herself.

But what she did do—much to her own dismay—was become instantly aware all over again that he was jaw-droppingly handsome and brought with him a heady, primitively sensual masculinity that alerted everything female inside her.

Not that she was going to let that make any difference to her. Now that she knew what he was made up of.

"I need a few questions answered," he informed her bluntly as he closed the door behind him.

"So you said," Megan answered in the same stern voice he was still using on her.

"Mind if I sit down?" he asked, pointing with a nod of his head to the chair around the corner from her at the square oak table her father had made by hand.

"Suit yourself," was Megan's curt reply.

But for some reason, her response seemed to amuse him. He was fighting it, but a smile tugged at the corners of his mouth just the same.

"Are we getting defensive here?" he asked then.

"Since you seem to want to treat me like some kind of criminal, I guess *we* are, yes."

He shot a glance at the wrist of the hand she was using to grasp her teacup and said, "I don't see any handcuffs and I haven't hauled you into the station. How am I treating you like a criminal?"

"Your attitude."

"My attitude. My attitude is that I've just found a

body buried in your backyard and I have some questions about it. I don't think that's unreasonable."

"I haven't lived here since I was twelve years old. What do you expect me to know about it?"

"Twelve years old, huh? My brother Scott is thirty and he was in your class in elementary school. That'd mean you and your family moved away eighteen years ago, right?"

"Has the interrogation begun?"

That made him chuckle. Clearly at some point he'd begun to enjoy himself.

"I don't think this could be considered an interrogation. But that *is* one of my questions, yeah."

"Eighteen years ago—yes, that's when my family left Elk Creek," she supplied what was no secret.

"What month?"

"June. Right after school let out for the summer."

"What do you remember about that time?"

Megan rolled her eyes. "This is just silly."

"Humor me," he suggested, his tone cajoling now.

She took a deep breath and decided it wasn't going to do anyone any good to go on being hostile. Besides, Josh Brimley was getting too much pleasure out of it and she didn't want to contribute to that.

So, after a sigh, she said in a calmer tone, "What I remember about June, eighteen years ago, is that I didn't want to leave. That my parents had turned an old school bus into a mobile home so we could live on the road going from one cause to another because they'd decided that being here was basically living with their heads in the sand and they couldn't go on doing that when there were so many social and environmental injustices that needed to be addressed. They wanted to be active, not passive, and that meant not staying in Elk Creek."

"How about the exact month you left? Do you remember anyone being around besides your mother and father?"

"My sister."

"Anyone besides your mother, father and *sister?*" he amended.

"No."

"Think about it."

"I don't have to think about it. I don't remember anything except not wanting to go."

Josh Brimley's navy-blue eyes stayed on her, as if he knew better and would stay in a stare-down with her until she told him the truth.

But that *was* the truth—she didn't recall anything but being miserable at the thought of leaving her home to live in a bus and be taught by her mother rather than staying in one place and going to school like everyone else.

Maybe her continuing silence finally convinced Josh that she didn't have any more to say on the matter because after a few moments he seemed to decide to make an attempt at sparking her memory rather than merely waiting her out.

"What about friends your parents might have had or maybe an uncle or a cousin? Do you remember anyone like that being around?"

"Neither of my parents have a brother and even if they did, both their families steer clear of them because they think my folks are lunatics. And as for friends, what I *do* remember was that there weren't a lot of people around Elk Creek who my parents were close enough to to call friends. Their friends then and now are other people like them."

"Okay, they didn't have a lot of friends around town—that's one thing more that you've remembered than you had a minute ago. Keep thinking about it. Did they maybe have a visit from a friend from somewhere else? Maybe who was here and then gone just before you left?"

"I don't remember anyone. It was a long, *long* time ago. Do you remember who might have been around your house when you were twelve? Who your parents hung out with? Go ahead, June, eighteen years ago—tell me what you remember about it."

Josh held up both hands, palms outward as if to ward off an attack. "Okay, point taken," he conceded.

"Finally," Megan said on another sigh.

"But I'm going to need to talk to your folks," he said then.

"I know you'll probably see this as my being uncooperative," she prefaced. "But talking to my folks is easier said than done. They're on board a ship off the coast of Peru trying to stop the dumping of waste solvents. It isn't as if I can just pick up the phone and reach them."

"How can they be contacted?"

"There's a number I can call to have word sent out to the ship and then my parents will have to contact me when they can."

"Then that's what you'll have to do."

Just like that, Megan thought. He gave the order and she was supposed to follow it.

But she'd had a lifetime of role models who bucked authority at every turn and it wasn't easy for her not to follow in those same shoes. Something about just the way he'd given the order made her feel contrary.

"I don't see why I should have to bother them," she said. "My parents didn't have anything to do with whatever happened here any more than I did."

"There's someone buried in your backyard," Josh said with forced patience, explaining the obvious and then adding to it. "And in the grave, along with the skeleton, is a newspaper dated June, eighteen years ago. That puts the time of death at the exact month, the exact year that your parents hightailed it out of town. Those are a whole lot of reasons why I need to talk to them."

"They didn't *hightail it out of town.* They left because of a strong social conscience and a belief that they could make a difference in the world. Nowhere in that are they the kind of people who would bring harm to another human being, let alone bury them in their backyard and *hightail it out of town.*"

"Even good people can do bad things under certain conditions, Megan."

She tried not to like the way her name sounded being said by that deep voice of his for the first time.

"My parents don't do bad things under any conditions. They wouldn't even hurt a fly. In fact, if one gets indoors, they chase it around until they can catch it in a cup and set it free outside. They've protested for the rights of people who are being abused or neglected or treated in any way unfairly. They're *against* doing bad things."

"I understand that it's impossible to believe the worst of your own family. But the fact is, someone was buried in your backyard at the same time your parents opted to take to the road. Now that may be circumstantial, it may be purely coincidental, but I'll still need to talk to them about it."

"Without condemning them with premature conclusions," she said as if it were a condition she was applying.

"I'm not condemning anyone and I don't have any premature conclusions. I'm just beginning at the beginning."

She couldn't refute that reasoning, even though the contrary part of her still wanted to. Besides, she knew when she'd lost a fight.

But that didn't mean she was just going to roll over without getting a little something in return.

So she said, "Say please."

"Say please?" he repeated, sounding partially amused again and partially in disbelief of what he was hearing.

Then he leaned across the corner of the table, putting his extraordinarily handsome face within inches of hers. They were almost nose to nose and he was near enough for her to smell the lingering scent of his aftershave and a sweetness on his breath as he said, "In case it's escaped you, I'm the law around here. I don't have to say please when it comes to this. If you don't do what I tell you to do I can charge you with obstruction and put your little fanny in jail."

Megan angled her chin upward in answer.

It was an act of defiance. But what she hadn't factored in was that that act of defiance also accidentally put her mouth in close proximity to his. So close that it suddenly occurred to her that he could kiss her without much more effort.

And the trouble with that realization was that once it was there in her head, it left her unable to think about anything else.

Until she reminded herself that they were in the middle of a tug-of-war.

"Say please anyway," she insisted.

Josh smiled. A slow, leisurely smile that was oh-so-sexy and made her wonder if he'd just read her thoughts.

Or maybe he was on the verge of arresting her and looking forward to it.

Then he said, "Please," in a husky whisper that gave her goose bumps.

She rubbed her arms as if she'd caught another chill, worried that he might see the gooseflesh.

"I'll do what I can," she finally conceded as if she didn't have a single other thing on her mind.

But Josh didn't back away even after he had her word. He stayed leaning across the table.

And the longer he did, the more those thoughts of kissing gained strength. Strength and potency and vividness as she began to wonder what it might be like to have him actually do it. To have him kiss her…

Then, abruptly, Josh stood and went to the door.

Megan didn't move to follow him, to walk him out, because she was struggling to regain the equilibrium she seemed to have lost in those thoughts of him kissing her.

"I'll need to talk to your parents right away so make sure you get on it ASAP. Please," he added with the hint of yet another smile.

"I'll put in the initial call tonight," she told him without a fight this time because she was locked in her own internal battle against this wholly inappropriate and unwarranted reaction to the man.

"Thanks," he said. "I'll be in touch."

Oh great, now she was thinking about him *touching* her, too....

Megan managed a nod as she watched his big hand close around the knob to open the door again.

Then, as if he'd just had a flash of memory, he said, "Don't do anything to the grave site. I'll need clearance from forensics before it can be tampered with or filled in."

Once more Megan nodded, not speaking as she marveled at all he was still inspiring in her even now.

He hesitated a moment as if he had something else to say. But in the end he went out the way he'd come in, closing the door behind him and leaving Megan alone in the kitchen again.

When she was, she breathed another sigh, this one a deep sigh of relief to be out from under the powerful effects of his presence.

And that was when rational thought kicked in again.

Was there anything dumber than getting carried away by a man who not only thought she was some kind of oddity, but who also seemed to think her parents were capable of something as awful as killing someone? she asked herself.

No, there wasn't anything dumber than that.

But that's what had just happened, hadn't it? In the middle of him questioning her and trying to find information that incriminated her family, she'd been imagining Josh Brimley kissing her. Josh Brimley who had accused her of practicing hocus-pocus and voodoo.

It was worse than dumb. It was insane.

And it wasn't going to happen again, she told herself firmly.

Josh Brimley was not just some nice guy she'd met in passing. In a way he was the enemy and she'd better not lose sight of that fact.

She'd better not lose sight of what kind of man he was.

Because while she might have faith that she could win over Elk Creek's citizens to the benefits of acupuncture, she knew better than to put any effort whatsoever into trying to convince a man who viewed her as an oddity that that wasn't what she was. And when that man also suspected her parents of a horrible crime on top of it, she really knew he was someone to stay away from.

The trouble was, loitering around the edges of her mind was the last view she'd had of Josh Brimley walking out the door.

The view of a rear end to die for.

And no matter how hard she tried, she couldn't shake off her appreciation of that....

Chapter 3

"WHEN'RE YOU GONNA DO somethin' 'bout them allergies, boy?"

Josh held up his hand in acknowledgement of his mother speaking to him as he sneezed three more times. Merely walking into the kitchen the next morning and being in the proximity of the mudroom where his brothers hung their work coats was enough to send him into a paroxysm of sneezing.

When it finally subsided, he said, "I don't have the time to do something about it now."

He hadn't told even his mother about his appointment the previous day with Megan Bailey and her needles. And certainly now there were more important issues that needed to be dealt with.

"You got in awful late last night and you're up even earlier than usual this mornin'," Junebug observed then, as Josh poured himself a cup of coffee. She sat at the kitchen table with her own mug and the romance novel she read a few pages of each day since she was up before the newspaper arrived.

"Something's happened," Josh answered as he joined

her. Then he went on to explain the discovery of the grave on Megan Bailey's property.

When he'd given his mother all the details—except for the fact that he'd been about to undergo acupuncture when Burt Connor had found him—Josh said, "Anything you remember about the Baileys from way back?"

Apparently there was, because Junebug turned down the corner of one page in her book and closed it as if she knew she wasn't going to be reading any more of it.

"Not likely to forget those people," she told Josh then. "They weren't like anybody else around these parts."

"I know they're environmentalists," he supplied.

"If that's what you call it. Most folks called it rabble-rousin' and trouble-makin' and worse. They turned that farm of theirs into one of them communes for a while before they had kids. There were rumors of free love and drug-takin' and who knows what all goin' on."

"Really?" Josh said, interested to hear what his mother was saying. "What happened after they had kids?"

"No more communal livin' with the slew of long-haired, smelly sorts they had there before. But even after that they'd let just any passerby into their house. It's one thing to be neighborly and friendly and hospitable to folks if you know 'em or if you know somebody else who knows 'em. But the Baileys, they'd take in vaga-bonds and riffraff, anybody."

"Do you remember anyone like that in particular? Around eighteen years ago?"

Josh's mother was an enormous woman—six feet tall and three hundred pounds. Her hair was pure white and she wore it pulled into a bun on the top of her head, leaving every inch of her meaty face exposed for the look she gave her son that said he was out of his mind.

"Do I remember who might have been hangin' around the Bailey place eighteen years ago? 'Course not. It wasn't like I visited with 'em. They alienated themselves from folks around here."

"How did they do that?"

"Mostly by not eatin' meat."

"A lot of people don't eat meat," Josh pointed out, suppressing a smile at his mother's horror at the very notion.

"Not back when they were around. But even then nobody woulda cared what they ate or didn't eat except that they made it known that they objected to the raisin' of animals for food. That didn't make 'em popular in ranch country. Plus they picketed around town and made more'n one scene at Margie Wilson's Café and over at the Dairy King. Then there was some vandalizing of the slaughterhouse that everybody knew had to be them even though the sheriff at the time couldn't prove it."

Junebug paused a moment, as if something had just occurred to her.

Amidst more sneezing, Josh hoped for a breakthrough, some flash of memory about someone or something that had gone on at the Bailey place eighteen years ago.

But that wasn't what he got. Instead his mother said, "Come to think of it, it doesn't really fit that they'd be involved in hurtin' a person when they were so set against any harm comin' to any livin' thing. They thought eatin' an egg was a crime against nature."

"That's what their daughter says about them, too."

"Pretty girls, those Bailey daughters. I saw 'em in town the other day. Which of 'em were you talkin' to?"

"Megan. The one Scott knows."

"The acupuncture one?"

"Yeah."

That's all he said—*yeah.* And something about it was enough to raise his mother's bushy white eyebrows.

"What about the other one? Did you do any talkin' to her?" Junebug asked as if she were testing him.

"I didn't meet the other one. She didn't come home the whole time I was at their place overseeing the removal of the evidence."

"But you liked the acupuncture one well enough."

It was a statement of fact, not a question, and even though Josh was a grown man his mother still surprised him with how easily she could see through him.

"I didn't find anything to dislike about her," he answered, making sure to sound completely noncommittal. "But my job isn't to like or dislike her. My job is to find out how and why someone was buried in her backyard eighteen years ago, the same month her family moved out of Elk Creek."

A slow, knowing grin spread across Junebug's face. "Oh, you liked 'er all right."

Josh just rolled his eyes and forced the subject back to the matters at hand. "What about anybody around here disappearing suddenly, eighteen years ago? Do

you remember anything like that? Maybe someone connected with the slaughterhouse? Or to something else
the Baileys were opposed to?"

"Nah." Junebug confirmed what Millie had told him
the night before about the lack of missing persons cases
in town. "Besides, if somethin' like that had ever happened 'round here there'd still be talk and you'd of heard
it already yourself."

That was true enough. Stories in Elk Creek were told
over and over through generations.

"But if the Baileys took in passers-by," Josh reasoned,
"there could have been someone there who no one else
knew or took notice of. Or would have thought twice
about when they weren't around anymore."

"S'pose so. Here today, gone tomorrow, there were
a lot of folks like that with the Baileys. But then there's
always been ranch hands or crop-pickers who've come
in and left again without much ado. It's just that the
Baileys were the only ones to open their doors to even
the disreputable sorts who happened through."

Josh nodded, taking a mental note of the picture his
mother was painting of the Baileys and realizing that it
didn't make his job any easier.

Then he said, "And there isn't anything else you can
think of that might help?"

Junebug shrugged her beefy shoulders. "Sorry." Then,
as if that were far less important than the interest she
thought her son had in Megan Bailey, she said, "Maybe
you ought to try that acupuncture for your allergy."

Josh pretended that was the farthest thing from
his mind.

"Couldn't hurt," Junebug persisted.

"Having needles stuck in me? What about that do you think couldn't hurt?" he scoffed.

"They say it's painless."

"Who says?"

"I've just heard. Besides, you could stare into that Megan Bailey's pretty face and I'll bet you wouldn't even feel the pain."

"I have an investigation into an eighteen-year-old crime on my hands. I don't have time for whatever it is you're tryin' to encourage here."

"Investigatin' a body in her backyard'll give you the chance to see 'er. Talk to 'er. Get to know 'er. Havin' her do acupuncture, that would be another way. You keep to yourself too much ever since Farrah did wrong by you. Time you get out there again."

Josh finished his coffee and took his cup to the sink. "I think for now I'll just tend to business, if that's all right with you."

Junebug didn't say another word as Josh suffered through one more sneezing attack.

But once it was over and he headed out of the kitchen to get to work, he caught her smiling that knowing smile again.

Only this time it irritated him to no end.

"How did a Ladies' League meeting and dinner turn into something that kept you out so late I fell asleep waiting for you?" Megan asked her sister Annissa when Annissa got out of bed at eight the next morning and came into the kitchen where Megan was having tea and toast.

"Didn't you get the message I left on the answering machine?" Nissa countered with a question of her own.

"I got it but all you said was you'd had a good response to the chair massages and didn't know when you'd get here. What exactly does that mean? The Ladies' League had you doing chair massages until after midnight?"

Nissa laughed as she made herself a cup of herbal tea. "No, but I was a big hit there. So big that Kansas Heller suggested that if I was interested in drumming up even more business I should take the chair to her husband's honky-tonk one night and do a few free massages there, too. You know, The Buckin' Bronco, over by the train station? She said I'd be introducing the massages to a whole different contingent and broaden my customer base. I thought she was right and that I should strike while the iron was hot, so when she offered to take me over right then, I accepted."

"And you were a big hit there, too," Megan guessed.

"I handed out every card and coupon I had with me and then started writing our office phone number and the ten-percent-off deal on bar napkins. And all the while I talked about the good acupuncture can do, too. I know it was unconventional but I really think I drummed up some business yesterday and last night."

"Great."

Nissa moved to the kitchen sink to set the tea ball in it to drain just as Megan said, "I had a pretty amazing night myself."

"What in the world…"

Nissa wasn't commenting on what Megan had said. Megan knew that her sister had just caught sight of the crime scene tape around the hole that stood between the house and the dilapidated barn out back. It was the opening Megan had been waiting for and she finally filled Nissa in on the events of the previous evening.

When she'd finished, she said, "Do you remember anything unusual about the time just before we left here? Anything that might help identify who the man was or what happened to him?"

Nissa shrugged and shook her head at once. "No. I remember the two of us crying because we didn't want to go and not liking the idea of living on a bus, but that's about all. It was a long time ago."

"My point exactly! But Josh Brimley refuses to see that."

"And he's convinced Mom and Dad had something to do with whatever happened?" Nissa asked, referring to that portion of what Megan had told her.

"So convinced that if they were here now I think he'd have them locked up already," Megan confirmed.

"That's just crazy. They wouldn't hurt anyone."

"Also what I told him. His only answer was that it's hard for people to believe the worst of their family."

"That's true, but still, Mom and Dad wouldn't hurt a flea, let alone another human being."

"Josh Brimley isn't going to take your word any more than he took mine."

"Did you put the call in to Peru?" Nissa asked as she

came to sit at the table with Megan, in the same chair Josh Brimley had occupied the evening before.

The same chair Megan had spent too much time this morning staring at and picturing him in the night before. All handsome and muscular...

And suspicious. Don't lose sight of *that,* she told herself.

"I called the number the folks gave us if we needed to reach them," Megan said when she'd leashed her thoughts. "But there's no telling how long it will take to get the message out to them and arrange long-distance ship-to-shore contact. The person I spoke to warned me that it could be days."

"I don't suppose the sheriff will be happy to hear that."

"You can bet on it." Of course he *had* shown a little pleasure in certain things the previous evening, but none of them had had to do with being denied his requests or a delay in doing his bidding.

"Had you done his acupuncture before all this happened?" Nissa asked then.

"No, he was in the process of telling me that he thought it was hocus-pocus or voodoo or something."

"Ah, he's one of those."

"It didn't bother me at first. I thought he was just being honest about his skepticism, and that I'd win him over. But later... Well, he made me mad with his barely veiled accusations of Mom and Dad, and I changed my mind."

Nissa laughed. "It bothered you belatedly?"

"Something like that. But by then everything about him bothered me."

"Oh?" There was a lilt in her sister's tone that made Nissa seem more interested in that than in anything else they'd been talking about. "What else about him bothered you?"

"His tunnel-vision. His close-mindedness. The fact that he has a basketful of preconceived notions about me and acupuncture and our whole family—including that Mom and Dad could be murderers, of all things. He's definitely what I swore to myself I'd never get involved with again after Noel, that's for sure."

"Were we talking about you getting involved with him?"

"No, I'm just saying—"

"But obviously the thought occurred to you."

Her sister knew her too well and Megan realized there was no sense in denying that the vague thought of some fleeting kind of involvement with Josh Brimley had flitted through her mind.

"Okay, maybe, just in passing," she conceded. "He's a great big, good-looking guy. It would have occurred to anyone."

"So you *were* attracted to him."

"I wouldn't say *attracted*, no. I just did some objective observation."

"And came to the conclusion that he was a great big, good-looking guy," Nissa repeated, teasing her now.

"That's not a conclusion I needed to come to. It's an empirical fact."

"An empirical fact that you took note of."

"Do you want to talk about the problems this man is determined to cause us or about his appearance?"

"Maybe you could flirt us out of problems with him," Nissa joked.

"You definitely don't know Josh Brimley." Although there *had* been some flirting going on in the undercurrents.

Or had she only imagined it? Maybe at the same time she'd been imagining him kissing her...

"This is serious, Nissa," Megan claimed as if her own mind hadn't just wandered from the weightiness of the situation. "I don't think it's a good idea to take it lightly."

Nissa shrugged again. "No matter how we take it, what can we do about it? I assume this Josh Brimley is going to investigate and find out what really happened all those years ago and who did it."

"But will he find out the truth if he doesn't look at any scenario that doesn't put the blame on Mom and Dad? Because as it stands now, he seems to believe that our leaving Elk Creek was a sign of their guilt, that they were running away."

"I have to think that the truth will out," Nissa said, honestly sounding unconcerned as she took her cup and headed for the shower.

But Megan couldn't be so confident. She didn't for a minute doubt her parents' innocence. But she did doubt that Josh Brimley would explore other possibilities since he'd seemed to have his heels dug into suspecting them.

So what was she going to do about it? she asked herself.

But she didn't have an instant answer.

Especially not when that kitchen chair Nissa had just vacated started taunting her with images of the sheriff sitting in it again.

And once that happened, she had trouble concentrating on anything else....

When Josh Brimley showed up at her office at about the same time that afternoon that he had the afternoon before, Megan's first thought was that he must have been passing by, seen her through the waiting room windows putting the final touches on the baseboard paint and decided that even though it was Sunday he might as well take advantage of her being there and come in to have the acupuncture they hadn't gotten to the previous day. She even imagined that he'd reconsidered everything, realized how silly he was being to suspect her parents of murder, opened up his mind to an alternative allergy treatment, and they could start fresh.

Okay, so maybe she was being naive and overly optimistic. But she certainly didn't expect what he'd really come for.

"You have a warrant to search our house and belongings?"

"That's what I said. I'll need you to take us over there and let us in right now."

"Us?"

He nodded his handsome head over his shoulder and for the first time Megan noted the forensics van that had been at her house the prior evening and a State Patrol car parked on the opposite side of Center Street near Josh's squad car.

"You can't be serious," she said in clear disbelief.

"As serious as I can get," he assured her. "It's standard operating procedure. The forensics guys want another look around in daylight and the patrolmen and I need to search the house and premises. I had to go into Cheyenne and interrupt a judge's Sunday dinner to get the warrant but I didn't have any problem convincing the judge that it should be issued and executed immediately."

"Right. On a Sunday. Before Nissa and I might destroy evidence that's already been around for eighteen years."

"It's just routine."

"For you to go through our things?" Megan said as the reality of a home search began to sink in.

Josh's silence confirmed that he was. "You're welcome to just give me the key and stay here so you don't have to see it."

That was even worse.

"You can't go into my house without me at least being there."

"It's up to you. But one way or another I'm already slowing things down by coming here first to let you know. I have to get out there."

Was that supposed to make her feel better? That he was allowing her some small courtesy he wouldn't have allowed someone else before he rifled through her underwear drawer?

Well, it *didn't* make her feel better about it. Not in the least.

But regardless of how she felt, when she glanced at the warrant he handed her as proof of what he was saying, she could see she didn't have a choice in the matter.

"I guess I'll have to take you," she finally said, wishing her sister were there to go along. But Nissa had garnered more than interest from potential clients the previous night and had gone on a date to Cheyenne for the day and evening. Which left Megan alone on the hot seat.

"We'll mainly be looking for blood," Josh told her. "On the walls, the floors, the baseboards, the doorjambs, the edges and corners of counters and cupboards, and on whatever furniture has been there all along. We'll probably have to spray luminol inside the drawers of any dresser that you didn't bring with you, but you can take out your personal things yourself before we do that. And on the bright side, for now the warrant doesn't allow us to pull up floorboards or get into your pipes."

He seemed to think that was some kind of consolation. He also almost sounded sympathetic and apologetic. But none of it made any difference. A bunch of strangers—*men*—were about to go into her home, open her closet doors, her cupboards, her drawers, and go through every nook and cranny of her living quarters, no matter how private. There was no consolation for that and even if he was sorry about it, it didn't change anything.

But since there was nothing she could do to stop it,

Megan closed her paint can, went to set her brush to soak in the sink in the break room and, without another word to Josh Brimley, she walked out of her office to her car, thinking the whole way that no matter how terrific-looking Josh Brimley was, it didn't make up for this.

The search took several hours and Megan hated every minute of it. Even though Josh allowed her to be the one to take her and Nissa's undergarments from the drawers, and their personal things from the bathroom, he was still right there watching her, keeping an eye on everything she removed as she removed it.

It was humiliating. Embarrassing. Enraging.

And it made her determined to dish out a little in return. So, once her and Nissa's unmentionables were out of the way, she opted for never letting Josh out of her sight as if she didn't trust him as far as she could see him.

But it didn't seem to bother him quite the same way. Instead, as if she weren't there at all, he went about his business.

As the forensics unit studied the grave and surrounding area, and the patrolmen walked the rest of the property and searched the old barn, Josh searched the house.

He did a thorough job of it, beginning by getting up into the attic and down into the crawl space, then turning his attention to the main floor and the second level of the two-story home.

Since the furniture had been there from before her family had taken to the road, Josh left no piece of it unmoved, overturned, or with a drawer that wasn't pulled completely free and checked inside and out.

When that was accomplished, he sprayed the luminol over nearly every surface and used a fluorescent light that he explained would expose even old blood that was invisible to the naked eye.

And while he confiscated several items—her father's ancient sneakers and her mother's equally aged gardening gloves among them—Megan was convinced he didn't find anything that would end up being evidence of a crime.

It was after eight o'clock that evening before Josh decreed the search over. The forensics men had left before sundown but the other two officers had stayed as long as Josh.

Megan could see them through the living room window, talking beside the patrol car. She wondered if they were all just going to leave or if at least one of them would allow her the courtesy of a goodbye.

She didn't have long to wonder, though. After a while Josh shook both men's hands and watched them get in their car.

But he didn't follow suit. Instead he stayed staring after them until they'd driven out of sight.

Then he retraced his steps back to the house and came in without so much as a knock on the front door that opened into the living room.

Still, he didn't say goodbye. He didn't say anything. He merely leaned a nonchalant shoulder against the

door he'd closed behind himself and gave Megan the
once-over.

"Time for my strip search?" she said facetiously
before she realized what she was actually saying.

Josh cracked a smile—the first since he'd shown up
at her office that afternoon—and raised a charmingly
lascivious eyebrow at her. "Are you offering?"

Megan could feel her face heat and knew it was turning cherry-red—a hazard of having such a fair complex-
ion. "I just meant that that seems like the only thing you
haven't done here, so I'm wondering if that's what I'm in
store for since you didn't leave with the rest of them."

She was only making it worse and she knew it, so
she finally stopped talking.

Josh's smile remained, as if he were still enjoying
her blunder and the blush it had induced. "As a matter
of fact, I'm off the clock now and I thought I'd help get
everything back in place."

"Oh," she said for lack of a better response as his big
hands began to roll up the cuffs of his uniform shirt,
exposing thick wrists and hair-spattered forearms.

Helping to put everything back in place was a nice
thing for him to do but it left Megan in a melee of mixed
feelings.

She was mad at him for this whole thing. For suspecting her parents. For searching her home.

But at the same time, here she was feeling pleased by
his offer to pitch in with the cleanup and admiring the
sight of oh-so-masculine hands and wrists and arms, of
all things.

Of course it had been that way all afternoon and

evening. Even in the midst of invading her privacy not a detail about him had escaped her notice.

She'd taken in every scuff on his cowboy boots, and the snug caress of blue jeans that fitted his to-die-for derriere like kid gloves. She'd studied his uniform shirt—a tan color with darker brown epaulets and flaps on the breast pockets. She'd surreptitiously read the lettering on the sheriff's department insignias that rode each of the sleeves where his biceps stretched them to their limit. She'd memorized the number on the badge emblazoned on a chest that appeared to be made up of massive pectorals. And all in all she couldn't help but be aware of how incredibly appealing he looked. Despite the fact that he was tossing her home as if she were a common criminal.

"So what do you say? Let's put this place back in order."

For a moment more Megan just stared at him. He'd been freshly shaved when he'd shown up at her office and she could still smell the faint scent of a sea breeze-like aftershave wafting to her from where he stood.

Tell him no thanks, she ordered herself. *Tell him that if his business is finished he should get out, that he isn't welcome here.*

But the trouble was, as much as she knew she *should* say exactly that, she couldn't quite do it.

Instead, another voice somewhere in her head said, *He was the one who made the mess, he should be the one to clean it up....*

And somehow that seemed perfectly reasonable.

"Where would you like to start?" she heard herself say suddenly.

"How about in the same order I messed things up? You can put your things back in the bathroom and the dresser drawers while I get the beds and bureaus against the walls again."

Megan was about to agree when her stomach rumbled quietly and reminded her how hungry she was.

"Or you could go to work on the furniture and I could make us a couple of sandwiches," she suggested.

"Better yet. It's way past suppertime and I'm starving."

And wasn't this all amiable and companionable? Megan thought, feeling disloyal.

But again there was emotional confusion because she was also feeling a twinge of excitement at the prospect of the two of them sharing a light, impromptu supper alone together.

This was really crazy, she decided, wondering if she should rescind her own offer of sandwiches, reject his offer of help putting the house in order, and call it a night after all.

Only once more she just couldn't bring herself to do it.

It would be rude, she rationalized. Not to mention that being on the good side of the sheriff seemed wiser than alienating him any more than she already had.

It didn't mean she was any less resentful of his suspicions of her parents or any less on their side. It was just good public relations, she assured herself.

"Sandwiches," she repeated as if to remind herself.

"Furniture," Josh said the same way.

Then he pushed off the door and spun around to the staircase.

And only when his eyes slid away from her then did she realize he'd been watching her very intently. So intently that it was almost as if she'd been under a heat lamp. A heat lamp that had just been turned off.

It was a strange sensation. Especially since it was accompanied by the slight wave of disappointment she was experiencing, as well as the desire to regain the warmth of that midnight-blue gaze in whatever way she could.

Crazy. Definitely crazy.

"Food," Megan whispered to herself, again in reminder.

Maybe she hadn't gone crazy, she thought then. Maybe hunger had made her go haywire. Maybe as soon as she got something in her stomach she'd be more resistant to Josh Brimley's effects.

And it was with the hope that that was true that she forced herself into motion and went to the kitchen.

It took nearly forty-five minutes for Megan to get the sandwiches ready. The search had left her kitchen in as much disarray as the rest of the house and she had to clear space among the dishes, pots and pans, utensils, and even foodstuffs that had been left out of cupboards, drawers and pantry to litter the countertops and kitchen table.

But even after making room to prepare their food there still wasn't anywhere to eat it so, when she finished, she decided they'd have to dine picnic-style in the living room, around the coffee table.

With that in mind, she piled everything on a tray and pushed through the swinging door that connected the kitchen to the living room.

Josh was already in the living room, pushing the sofa against the wall facing the front door and the picture window. It was the last of the furniture to be put back where it had been and once it was he took a quick scan of the room.

"All done," he announced just as Megan set the tray on the coffee table. "Upstairs and down. I think I have pretty much everything in order again. Except the books in that case in the upper hall. I thought you'd probably rather put them in whatever order they were in before and I didn't know what that was."

"I'll do it later, when I put things back in the drawers and clean the kitchen," Megan said. Then, glancing at the tray full of food, she added, "I thought we could eat in here."

"A picnic," he said as if he'd read her earlier thoughts.

"Mmm. The kitchen is in pretty bad shape."

"Sorry. But I think eating in here is a great idea anyway. I like things casual."

Megan knelt on the floor between the coffee table and the couch to set out the two food-laden plates, silverware, napkins and tall glasses of iced tea.

"Cloth napkins aren't too casual, though," Josh observed as he sat just around the bend of the oval table, also on the floor, with his back against the sofa and one leg bent at the knee to brace his forearm while his hand dangled over his shin.

"We don't use paper napkins. Cloth can be washed and reused. It's better for the environment," she explained.

"Ah."

He didn't say more on that subject and Megan appreciated his restraint.

"Big sandwiches," he said then, nodding toward his plate as he used his free hand to flip open the cloth napkin and lay it across the thigh of the leg he had extended out in front of him.

"The bread is seven grain, homemade," Megan explained. "Inside yours is a grilled portobello mushroom, tomato slices, roasted red peppers, artichoke hearts, black olives, onion, sprouts and a little vinaigrette."

Something about that made him smile at the same time his brow wrinkled up. "I'd have been happy with meat and mayo. This sounds like more trouble to go through than a sandwich deserves."

"Try it," she urged.

He looked skeptical but in a more congenial way than he had the day before when they'd talked about acupuncture. Still, he didn't dive in, though. It took him a moment of eyeing what was on his plate before he picked up one half of the three-inch-high sandwich. Then he gave it a meager taste, as if it might bite him back.

Megan waited for the verdict, watching him chew and pleased that it was with his mouth closed and without so much as a crumb on his supple lips.

Then he swallowed and his eyebrows rose. "It's good. Almost tastes like a steak sandwich."

Megan felt as if she'd finally won one small victory. She stretched out her own legs so she could sit more comfortably on the floor, too, and finally began to eat her own food.

"You told me what was inside *my* sandwich," Josh said then. "Does that mean there's something different in yours?"

"Turkey, ham and bacon," she answered with a straight face once she'd swallowed her own bite.

His responding expression was exactly what she'd been going for and she laughed at him.

"I'm kidding. Mine is the same as yours. Want to see?"

He grinned at her joke. "Last time a girl asked me that she wasn't talking about what was between two slices of bread."

Megan laughed at his innuendo but didn't give him the satisfaction of a comment.

Josh ate more sandwich, a few potato chips, and then poked his chin at the room in general. "Did I get the furniture pretty much back where you had it?"

Megan glanced around just to be sure. "Close enough."

"I didn't think I'd have a problem, that I'd just follow the marks on the floor. But there were other marks, too, so I wasn't sure in some spots. Looks like you did some rearranging when you moved in."

"We did."

"Seems better than it would have been if I'd followed the old marks. More open. It has a nice feel to it."

"Feng shui."

"I beg your pardon?"

"Feng shui is an ancient philosophy."

"An ancient philosophy of home decorating?"

"It's all about opening things up so there's a free flow of energy. When there's a free flow of energy you feel better and when you feel better everything is better. You said yourself that the room has a nice feel to it."

"You really believe that putting furniture in certain places will change your life?" he asked.

"I believe that anything that makes anyone more comfortable and content is a good thing. Even if that's all it does."

"Ah-ha! Then you admit it doesn't have any magical powers."

"I'm not admitting anything. I'm saying that if that's the least it does, it's worth it."

"And I suppose that crystal mobile you have in the corner over there is for a reason, too?"

"It helps direct the energy. Plus, I like the way it looks."

"Now that's something I can understand."

"So it's not mumbo-jumbo."

He had the good grace to laugh. "Yeah."

Megan just rolled her eyes at him.

"The sandwich was great, though," he said with a nod toward the plate he'd emptied several minutes earlier. "I never would have tried it on my own but I liked it."

"Even though there was no meat and mayo?"

"Even though."

"You get points for owning up to that, anyway."

He laughed again and Megan realized she was coming to like the sound of it. Probably too much.

"I didn't know you were keeping score," he said. "But I'll bet I can use all the points I can get."

"As a matter of fact," she teased.

"And I should probably leave while I'm ahead," he added, pushing himself to his haunches and standing from there.

Megan found herself awash in disappointment that he was leaving. But that fact alone—that she was disappointed—was enough to warn her she'd been enjoying his company too much. So, rather than protest, she stood, too, to walk him to the door.

"Oh, I almost forgot," he said along the way. "Did you try to reach your parents?"

Back to business. That was really disappointing.

"I put in the initial call this morning but it may be days before the connection can be made. All I can do now is wait for them to get the message and do a ship-to-shore call or dock somewhere."

They'd reached the front door by then and, with one hand on the knob, Josh turned to face her. "I need to hear from them as soon as possible. I hope you left that as part of the message."

"I did. But I think you need to be exploring other possibilities."

"What makes you think I'm not?"

"Oh, please. You have your sights set on them. Just because they don't live like most people and they're a little more radical than the average Mr. and Mrs. John Q. Public you believe they're automatically guilty."

"Right. It doesn't have anything to do with the evidence."

"Evidence or not, you need to be investigating other people."

"Do you have someone I should put on the suspect list?"

"No. I'm just saying that you have an obligation to keep an open mind, and I don't think that's what you're doing."

"So you're doubting my objectivity?" he said, but without any signs that that disturbed him.

"Yes, I am," she confirmed. "I'm worried that you've tried and convicted my parents already and that's that— you aren't even looking anywhere else."

"I wouldn't want to *worry* you," Josh said as if their entire conversation was amusing him. "Maybe you should tag along as I investigate just to make sure I leave no stone unturned."

If that was a challenge it was one she was going to take. "Maybe I should."

She met his midnight-blue eyes with her own and their gazes seemed to lock.

"You're welcome to," he said more seriously, his voice deeper.

"Then I will," Megan told him, her tone suddenly softer for no reason she could fathom. "When?"

"This case is all I'm working on. I'm going out to do interviews with your neighbors tomorrow."

"Tomorrow is fine. We could even do your acupuncture in the morning before and then head out."

That made his handsome face scrunch up and he broke off eye contact in the process, as if she'd suggested something unbearable.

"Maybe you're just afraid of the needles," Megan said then, goading him.

But it only made him chuckle once more. "Good bedside manner."

This time Megan had the grace to laugh before taking a better tack. "Give it a try. Just see if it doesn't work. I'll even make a deal with you—if it doesn't you don't have to pay me for the testing or the treatments."

His striking eyes caught hers again and there was pleasure in them that told her he was enjoying this as much as she was.

"Okay, deal," he agreed. "Tomorrow morning, first thing."

"And then I'm tagging along from there on your investigation."

"I wouldn't have it any other way," he said as if he were humoring her.

With everything settled and planned he should have left then. But he didn't. Instead he stayed there, still looking into her eyes.

And as they had the night before, thoughts of him kissing her popped into Megan's mind.

She told herself that really *was* crazy. That it was the very last thing she should be thinking about.

But there it was just the same. The thoughts. And worst, the wish that he would....

Then it seemed as if he actually might. It seemed as if he was leaning towards her a little. Maybe bending down.

She didn't mean to, but she tilted her chin ever so slightly upward and if he intended to kiss her, she would have been ready for it.

But then all of a sudden he straightened away from her and opened the door. Almost startling her because that was not what she was expecting.

"I'll be at your office at nine," he announced, his voice slightly husky, slightly gruff.

"I'll be there," Megan assured him, falling short of strengthening her own tone because she was still lost in what now seemed to have been merely imaginings that he might have been on the verge of kissing her.

Then he went out the door in a hurry, closing it behind him as if any less determined exit might not have been successful.

And Megan was left staring at the oak panel.

Staring at it and reaching a single hand to press her palm to it as if it were Josh's chest.

This will never do, she told herself, knowing without a doubt that she shouldn't be feeling what she was feeling or thinking what she was thinking.

But knowing it without a doubt and stopping it were two different things.

And she just couldn't stop thinking about what it might have been like if he *had* kissed her.

And wishing he had.

In spite of everything...

Chapter 4

BY THE TIME MEGAN opened the office the next morning she had a new determination about what could and what could not go on between herself and Josh Brimley when she saw him again.

No more noticing how great-looking he was. No more flirting or encouraging banter that brought out his quick wit. No more getting lost in the effects of his simmering sexuality. And definitely no more thinking about him kissing her. Or wishing he would.

He was a status quo kind of guy and no one knew better than she what that translated to in regards to a relationship with someone like her. It was something she needed to avoid at all costs. More so because of the whole criminal investigation he was engaged in.

What was between them had to be strictly business and nothing more.

Of course what was between them being anything more was quite possibly only in her imagination anyway. Which made her reaction to him even worse.

It chafed that she'd been ready to let him kiss her the evening before and he hadn't. But it was a sign she needed to pay attention to, she told herself for the ga-zillionth time since hearing his car drive off last night. Yes, it had seemed as if he might have been going to kiss her but even if that was the case, he'd stopped himself. Probably because, despite a little temptation, he wasn't interested in her as anything more than the daughter of his prime suspects. And that was something she'd better not forget.

Not that she was any more interested in him than he was in her, because she wasn't. She didn't know what had gotten into her these last two evenings as he was leaving but now that she knew those bizarre musings about kissing sneaked up on her, she was going to be on guard against them and make sure that it never happened again.

She really, really had learned her lesson with Noel. Opposites might attract but even when they did, it didn't work out in the long run. It was the things people had in common that bound them together. Differences only tore them apart.

And Megan couldn't go through that again. Not even for a big, strapping, exceptionally handsome guy like Josh Brimley.

No, she'd been down that road and at the inevitable end of it was too much pain. Pain she'd never put herself through again.

And that was all there was to it.

So it was good that he hadn't kissed her. It was good that he probably wasn't interested in her. It was good that she could head off whatever unwanted thoughts and images came into her own head from here on.

Because she and Josh Brimley were just not meant to be. She was sure of it.

She was going to make sure of it.

If it was the last thing she ever did.

That's how determined she was.

At the stroke of nine o'clock Megan was ready and waiting to do Josh's acupuncture.

But Josh didn't show.

He still wasn't there at nine-fifteen. Or at nine-thirty. Or nine-forty-five.

By ten she was convinced he wasn't coming at all and she began to think his agreeing to do the acupuncture before the two of them went out to talk to her neighbors about the skeleton had been a ruse. That he'd agreed to it exactly for this purpose—to get her to sit there and wait for him while he went on his interviews alone.

She was working up a full head of steam about being duped when the phone rang and Josh's voice came in answer to her, "Bailey Holistic Center."

"Megan? It's Josh. Look, I'm sorry I missed our appointment but there's been a change of plans for today."

"Oh?" she said icily, certain he was on the verge of telling her he'd had second thoughts about her overseeing his investigation and had gone out alone.

"I'm stuck at the office. Apparently word got around over the weekend about the grave in your backyard and I have a whole slew of folks already lined up to tell me what they think they know about it. It looks like I'll have to stay here all day and hear 'em out just in case there's something to what some of them have to say."

"Are you just making this up to get out of the acupuncture again?"

"You're welcome to keep the rest of our date today and come over to see for yourself. You can sit in on this stuff if you want to. But no, I'm not just pulling your leg to get out of the acupuncture. I'm swamped."

Megan's head of steam diffused and she fought the ridiculous skitter of something sensual that went through her at the thought of Josh *pulling her leg* in a more literal sense.

"So that's where you are? At your office? You haven't been out talking to people without me?"

"I haven't been out at all. I stopped in here on my way to your office to check on things, see if I had any messages, and there was already a whole group of people waiting for me. More have shown up since then and I've given up thinking I'm getting out of here any time today."

"And I can sit in on the interviews?"

"Be my guest. Millie is trying to get some kind of order going right now and then she'll start bringing them in. Come on over if you want."

"I'll be right there," she said without hesitation. "Don't talk to anybody else until I am."

She heard him laugh slightly. "Yes, ma'am," he said facetiously.

But Megan was in too much of a hurry to make amends for her tactless command. She was anxious to get to his office before he interviewed more people than it seemed like he already had.

So, rather than addressing her lack of tact, she merely hung up and charged out of her office.

Of course even as she did she didn't admit to herself that a large part of her eagerness and excitement was due to the fact that she was about to get to see Josh again.

But somewhere around the peripheries of her mind she knew it anyway.

Center Street was lined on both sides by picturesque old buildings that housed shops and small businesses. Some were clapboard, some brick. Some were one story, some two, and a few three. All were lovingly kept up and adorned with personal touches like bright blue awnings or gingham curtains in the windows or flower pots on the sills.

These quaint establishments ran the length of Elk Creek's long main thoroughfare until it turned into a circle drive around the town square. Then the buildings were larger and more austere—the tall steepled church, the red brick Molner Mansion that was now the town's medical facility, and the courthouse.

Like the Molner Mansion, the courthouse, too, was a red brick building. It stood a stately four stories high and was the site of the public works department, the post office, the mayor's office, the court, the city council meeting place, the sheriff's office and the jail—all two cells of it.

As Megan cut across the town square to get to the courthouse she could already see people standing in clusters around the entrance. It was as if the discovery in her backyard had prompted a social event.

Her approach caused a ripple of whispers—most of them about who she was—followed by silence as all eyes turned toward her.

Megan ignored her onlookers and went straight to the courthouse door. When she reached it one man opened it for her and she murmured a thank-you before going inside.

There were even more people filling the building's lobby, nearly surrounding the central information desk, standing around like reporters waiting for a news-break.

Their reaction to her was much the same as their outside counterparts and again Megan paid them little attention as she went to the sheriff's office—the first door on the left.

The small, stark office was also jammed from the door to the reception counter that cut the room in half. Behind the counter an extremely short, chubby woman with pewter-gray hair was shouting over the voices.

"Josh'll see you all in time. Just take one of these numbers I'm writin' on these pieces of paper and wait your turn."

"Are you Millie?" Megan asked when the older woman attempted to give her a number.

"'Course," the woman answered as if it were a silly question.

"I'm Megan Bailey," Megan said, hoping she wouldn't have to insist on seeing Josh out of turn.

She didn't. Millie did a double take, then said, "You can go on in."

"Thanks."

Megan squeezed through the crowd to get around the counter, into the clear space that ran from the back side of it to a gray metal desk she assumed was Millie's. The desk stood directly in front of a door where *Sheriff* was lettered on the glazed glass in the upper half. Megan knocked on the wooden frame that surrounded it.

"Yeah," came the impatient call from inside.

Megan opened the door only enough to slide through it before closing it again behind her.

"Be with you in a minute," Josh said from where he was standing at a file cabinet in the far corner of the room, looking through the top drawer.

His back was to her and since he didn't so much as glance over his shoulder to see who had entered his office, Megan was left with the rear view of him. Which meant impressively broad shoulders encased in another crisp uniform shirt, a torso that narrowed in a sharp V to his waist where his shirt was tucked into tight jeans, and that Greek god derriere that she suddenly imagined naked.

If anything was worse than imagining him kissing her, it was imagining his bare rear end, and Megan shuddered slightly at her own impropriety, yanking her gaze away and forcing herself to study the spare office instead.

His desk was an old wooden schoolteacher's desk with a plain, functional vinyl chair behind it. There was that sole gray metal filing cabinet he was still rifling through, two visitor's chairs in front of the desk, and an overstuffed tan sofa against the opposite wall. And that was about it. There weren't any pictures to corrupt the eggshell paint and the floor was covered by a serviceable indoor-outdoor carpet of industrial blue.

He did have a big window, though, that Megan guessed would look out onto Center Street if the blinds hadn't been pulled—probably to keep the gathering of townsfolk from watching what was going on in the office today.

Josh finally turned away from the filing cabinet.

He was freshly shaved and Megan caught a whiff of his aftershave. But she tried not to notice how nice it smelled. Just as she tried to stick to her guns about so many other things when it came to him. Like how exceptionally well put-together were the sharp angles and planes of his face. Like how tall and straight he stood. Like the fact that his eyes were piercing, and that merely being in that small room with him—even for the reason she was in that small room with him—made her feel more alive, more centered, more content, more complete...

Back to being crazy, she thought, working hard at regaining some semblance of her sanity.

"Good morning," she said in belated greeting then, her tone businesslike.

"Is it still only morning? Feels like I've already been here for hours."

"Have you seen that many people?" *Without me,* she wanted to add but she didn't.

"Half a dozen or so."

"Have they told you anything I should know?"

"Most of them were more interested in what they could get out of me in the way of gossip than in telling me anything."

"And the ones who had something to say?" Megan persisted.

He gave her a sly smile and answered with a question of his own, "Are you sure your parents are alive and well and the same people they were before you left Elk Creek?"

"Excuse me?"

"So far some of the theories I've heard are that your mother did in your father and ran off with another man, and that your father did in your mother and ran off with another woman."

"No, they're definitely alive and well and the same people they've always been."

"And seeing as how the skeleton is human we can rule out Merle Sutter's claim that your folks stole his blue-ribbon-winning horse Matilda, killed her in some heathen ritual—his words—and buried the bones in the yard." Josh scrunched up his handsome face, scratched the nape of his neck and said, "You can see how my day's gone so far."

"And there are so many more waiting to talk to you."

"Don't remind me. I think somebody declared today a holiday and forgot to tell me. Half the town seems to have taken the day off just to come in and solve this mystery for me."

"Only half?" Megan joked.

"Maybe two-thirds."

Josh seemed to actually see her for the first time then, giving her the once-over from top to toe to top again. "But you're looking like a little ray of sunshine," he said with a note of appreciation in his tone.

Okay, maybe she *had* paid particular attention to her appearance today. But not because of Josh, she'd assured herself. She'd opted for the bright yellow jumper that went over a white, long-sleeved under-dress because she hadn't wanted to meet her neighbors for the first time in so many years not looking cheery and put-together. And yes, she'd coiled her hair into a knot on the back of her head and jabbed two ornate chopstick-like skewers through it because she thought it gave her a somewhat more professional look. It hadn't had anything to do with Josh.

Even if he had popped into her mind a time or two—or three or four—along the way…

"I didn't want to look sloppy," she said in answer to his ray of sunshine comment.

"You definitely don't look sloppy. You look nice."

"Thanks," she said, wishing that didn't please her as much as it did. "Shouldn't we get started?" she asked when he went on studying her as if he'd forgotten that he was here to do a job and there were a lot of people waiting to see him.

"Sure," he said with what seemed to be a jolt out of some sort of reverie. Then he nodded toward the visitor's chairs. "Why don't you pull one of those around to the corner back here so you can see who I'm talking to. And I think we'd better set some ground rules."

"For who?"

"For you. My letting you be in on this is not by-the-book."

"If my parents were here they'd have the right to face their accusers."

"In court. Not in the initial interview. You're here just to satisfy yourself that I'm not overlooking anything that leads away from your parents. Period. And if it seems to me that someone is holding something back because you're here, I'm going to ask you to wait outside. And I want you to go without an argument. Is that clear?"

"What if I think you aren't delving deeply enough into something or that you're leaving an important question unasked?"

"I think I know how to do my job. But if there's something really important—and I mean *really* important—that you think I'm neglecting, I suppose you can pipe up a little. But what I don't want is for this to become some kind of campaign to convince anyone that your folks are innocent or to defend them against any remarks you might take offense to. If you get into any of that I'll do today's interviews—and the rest of the investigation—alone."

"You expect me to sit by and *not* defend my parents if they're being slandered and defamed?"

"I expect you to sit by and let me handle it. You have to know going in that there's likely to be some things said about your folks that won't make you happy. From what I've heard, they didn't really fit in around here and Elk Creek is just conservative enough to be automatically suspicious of things and people who are different than they are. Now, with a body turning up in your backyard, those suspicions are all going to come to the surface and seem to be legitimized. If you can't listen to what might be said about your family without debating it, you can't stay. You'll have to leave it to me to wade through what's just bias and what might be evidence."

"And you will be looking for leads in other directions," Megan said with a note of warning in her tone.

"I'll be looking for anything that seems pertinent. No matter who it's about or what it is. If you don't think you can handle that—"

"I know, I know, I can't stay," she said, letting him know she'd heard that edict enough. "Don't worry, I can handle it."

Josh stared at her another moment. But this time, rather than appreciation for how she looked, she read doubt in his expression.

"I'll be fine," she asserted, holding her head high.

He still didn't seem convinced but he finally took those midnight-blue eyes off her, pushed a button on the intercom on his desk, and said, "Okay, Millie, you can start sending 'em in." Then he released the button and those blue eyes returned to Megan. "Here we go. Come on back and make yourself comfortable."

Megan did just that, doing as he'd suggested and pulling one of his visitor's chairs to the corner behind Josh's desk and chair. From that position she could see the other visitor's chair that faced the desk and the back of Josh again as he also sat down.

It was either an opportune spot or a dangerous one and she had to remind herself to keep her focus off of the nape of his thick, strong neck where his hair was cut short and very precisely, as well as off his broad shoulders where they rose above his chair back.

After all, she lectured herself, she was, in essence, her parents' representative and she needed to pay attention to every detail of what went on in that room. Not to every detail of the town sheriff.

Then in came the first of the number holders and from that moment on even Josh was less of a distraction as one story or suspicion wilder than the next was woven.

It was no surprise that, as Josh had predicted, her family was what most people wanted to talk about. The fact that she was there to listen to it tempered some of what was said but it didn't stop it.

"All that peace, love and don't-hurt-the-animals was just a cover-up," was one claim. "Those Baileys were environmental terrorists hidin' from the authorities and that body in their yard was an FBI or a CIA agent that caught up with them."

"A cult," came another report. "It was a cult they ran out there. Keep diggin' and you'll probably find hundreds more bodies buried from a mass suicide."

"Free love ain't never as free as it sounds," one sanctimonious man informed them. "That's what was goin' on out there. Free love gone bad."

"They were fanatics about not eatin' meat," a local rancher's wife pointed out. "They acted like we were all heathens because we did. Everybody knew they tore up the slaughterhouse and that poor person buried at the

Bailey place was likely a hunter they took care of the same way."

Yet another opinion was, "It wasn't only pottery they were craftin', if you ask me. Look into the evil arts. Witchcraft's what they were probably practicin' and this has something to do with that. Mark my words."

There were accusations of an underground railroad for bad hippies. Mind control. One woman was certain she'd seen Megan's parents on *America's Most Wanted* at least three times. Another believed tofu killed a Bailey guest and they buried him in the yard rather than admit meat eating was healthier.

By the end of the day the only thing Megan knew with any certainty was that many of Elk Creek's citizens had very vivid imaginations.

She was grateful, though, for the way Josh dealt with it all. He wasted very little time on the absurd angles or ridiculous theories, and he cut every unflattering comment short. Instead he said over and over again that he was only interested in the facts.

But those were in short supply until long after the sun had gone down and Megan and Josh had lunched on sandwiches from Margie Wilson's Café and wolfed down a quick pizza supper between interviews.

It was nearly eight o'clock when Buzz Martindale dropped in just as they thought they might be able to call it a day.

Buzz was the grandfather of the McDermot family—who employed Josh's mother—and he came to let Josh know that he had a recollection of a drifter who had come through town at about the time Josh was interested in.

"I don't remember his name," the elderly man said. "And I couldn't tell you what happened to him. Like any drifter, he was here one day and gone the next. I just figgered he'd moved on. But what makes 'im stick in my mind was the rumor that he had two valuable coins of some kind. Coulda been nothin'. Coulda been somethin'."

"Can you describe him?" Josh asked.

"After all these years? A million faces passed before my eyes since then."

"Was he tall? Short? Thin? Fat?"

The older man thought about it. "Tall as me then— six feet. Not fat. Looked like he could use a good meal. The Baileys was folks likely to take in somebody like that, feed 'em. And if I'm not mistaken, that's where he spent his time. 'Round their place."

"How about the color of his hair? Or his eyes? Any scars or marks that might have made him memorable?" Josh persisted.

"Nope. Just the coins is all. And like I said, I never seen 'em or nothin'. Just heard talk about 'em. Don't know if they was made up or for real. But that's what I remember—a drifter stayin' out at the Bailey place moochin' off them people when he coulda sold them coins to help himself."

Buzz paused a moment as if something else was rising to the surface of his brain from deep below.

Then he said, "Wait a minute. His teeth. He was missin' one front tooth and most of the other. Uppers.

What was left of the partial one was pointy. That help any?"

"It might," Josh answered, taking notes on everything the old man was saying and sounding more interested than he had in anything else that had been said today.

"How about personal effects other than the coins?" he asked then. "Do you remember anything about his clothes or what he had with him?"

Buzz thought about it but then shook his head. "Sorry."

"Don't be sorry. This could actually help with an identification somewhere down the line."

And help to hang my parents, Megan thought.

But, as if the same thing occurred to Buzz Martindale and he didn't want it left that way, he said, "The Baileys were decent enough folks. Don't go thinkin' otherwise by what I said. They weren't the kind who'da took in some drifter so they could rob him of those coins and plant 'im in the yard. They had their peculiarities but those were all about savin' things, not hurtin' 'em."

Megan wanted to thank him for saying that but felt sure she wasn't supposed to do that any more than she was supposed to defend her parents.

"I just have to look into everything, Buzz," Josh said.

"Yeah, I know. That's why I came in to tell you what I recalled. But I'm not tellin' anybody else. Town's all het up over this already, convincin' itself that the Baileys were somethin' bigger'n life and badder'n bad when that just ain't the way it was. Not that it looks good for 'em, what with that body bein' on their property. But still, everybody deserves the benefit of the doubt."

"Thank you," Megan heard herself say, this time before she could curb the impulse.

Josh tossed a warning glance over his shoulder and then faced the elderly man who was laboriously pushing himself from the visitor's chair.

"That's all I got," Buzz announced then. "I just come into town to have supper with Bax and when I saw the light still on in here on my way home I thought I'd drop in and tell it to ya. Now I better git."

"I appreciate you coming in. If you think of anything else let me know," Josh said.

"Pretty sure that's all there is but anything else comes to me, you'll be the first I tell," the McDermot patriarch assured him. Then he nodded in Megan's direction to bid her goodbye. "Young lady."

"Good night," she countered, but it was to his retreating back.

Josh had taken notes during all the interviews, regardless of how farfetched the information, but this time he was more intent on the task, leaving Megan to her own devices without making any comment on what Buzz Martindale had reported.

But the silence in the office was not the only silence, Megan realized. The din of voices that had been coming both from outside the building and from outside the office since she'd arrived at the courthouse was missing, too.

"It's so quiet. Do you think Buzz Martindale was actually the last of them?" she whispered, as if saying it out loud might conjure up more people with something to say on the subject of her parents and the makeshift burial site in her backyard.

"I don't know. Poke your head out the door and see what Millie has to say about it."

Keeping her fingers crossed, Megan did just that, finding the diminutive older woman with her coat already on, taking her purse out of her desk drawer.

"Is that it?" Megan asked, again in a quiet voice.

"Thank the good Lord," Millie answered with gusto. "Tell Josh I'm goin' home and I'm comin' in an hour late tomorrow."

Whether he likes it or not was the implied finish to that statement. But no one could dispute the fact that the woman had earned more than an hour's delayed start after the day she'd put in. Besides, it was after eight o'clock—long past what Megan was sure was Millie's quitting time.

"I'll tell him."

Millie walked out then, without another word, and Megan turned back into the office to face Josh.

He'd apparently finished what he was writing because he was on his feet and in the middle of an elaborate stretch that had his long arms in the air, his spine arched and his torso bowed in a display so magnificent just the sight of it lit a tiny spark inside Megan.

"We're finished," she announced, going on to relay Millie's message in an attempt to keep herself on track and not get lost in watching Josh.

He relaxed from his stretch by slow increments and

even talk of Millie couldn't help Megan's eyes from
following every step of the way.

"Long day," he said when it was complete.

"And not all that productive," she felt obliged to point
out.

Josh didn't respond to that and there was a certain
amount of denial in his lack of confirmation.

But Megan realized suddenly that she was saturated
with the subject of this case and her parents' involvement—or lack of involvement—in it and so she didn't
push it.

Instead she said, "I should get going. Nissa will be
wondering what happened to me."

Why was there a question in her tone at the end of
that? Was she asking him to give her a reason to stay?

If she was it didn't matter because rather than doing
that Josh accepted her decision without argument. "Did
you drive over this morning?" he asked as if he were
only too willing to have her go.

"No, my car is still at my office. I walked over when
I got your call."

"Then how about if I walk you back?"

That was a much nicer proposition than what she'd
been thinking before—that he just wanted to get rid of
her.

But in an attempt to fight her own eagerness to pro-
long this already extended day with him, she said, "You
don't have to."

"I know I don't have to. But I've been cooped up here
for longer than I can tolerate and I could use the fresh
air."

So that's all he was interested in. It didn't have anything to do with her, Megan thought, her spirits riding a roller-coaster of ups and downs.

"Whatever," she said with a negligent shrug to go with her I-couldn't-care-less-what-you-do tone.

Josh's brow twitched into and out of a brief frown but he didn't say anything about her attitude. Instead he said, "We could go the long way around and pick up a couple of cups of hot chocolate at the Dairy King for the walk. My treat."

Again Megan's mood rose with the thought that he might want to spend some personal time with her. "That sounds good," she agreed even as she told herself to cut it out, that she shouldn't even be spending personal time with him, let alone hanging her heart on the possibility that he might or might not want to be with her.

But did she tell him to just forget it? To go have his hot chocolate by himself while she retrieved her car alone and went home?

No, she didn't.

What she did say was, "I'd love a cup of hot chocolate."

"Great. Then let's go before anyone else can drop in here to tell me they're sure Martians landed on your roof eighteen years ago and what we really found in your yard was the spacecraft."

"Mmm. That is about the only thing they didn't come up with today," Megan agreed with a small laugh.

Josh went around his desk to open the door on a closet on the inside wall, taking a short brown wool jacket from a hanger inside.

"Where's your coat?" he asked then, as if the thought had just popped into his mind.

"I ran out so fast this morning that I left that at my office, too."

Three strides of his long legs brought him to where Megan still stood at the door. "Here. Wear this or you'll freeze to death," he ordered, holding it open for her to slip into.

"If I wear it *you'll* freeze to death."

"Nah. The cold will feel good after this hot, stuffy office. I'll wear it on the way back, once you're in your car with the heater on."

He ignored her further protests and urged her into the jacket.

It was several sizes too big and Megan knew she must look ridiculous but as Josh ushered her out of the office she could smell his aftershave on the coat and the feel of it around her made her think about having his arms around her much the same way.

On guard, she reminded herself sternly. She was supposed to be on guard against the attraction to him sneaking up on her, against thoughts like that sneaking up on her. Against him. After all, it wasn't the walk or the hot chocolate that were potentially dangerous to her. It was her own thoughts. And the uninvited hope that went with them. And that couldn't go on. It had to be nipped in the bud.

So, determined to do just that, as soon as they stepped outside the courthouse building, she jabbed her nose skyward and took a deep draw of the cool night air, holding it in her lungs as long as she could before exhaling and hoping that was enough to clear her mind.

Josh misinterpreted the actions. "I know. Beautiful night, isn't it?"

"It is," Megan agreed as if that had been what was going through her mind the whole time.

The Dairy King was around the corner from the courthouse. Megan and Josh shared inconsequential small talk as they walked there, ordered two hot choco-lates and then headed across the town square again in the direction of Megan's office.

It was only once they were back on Center Street, sip-ping the sweet, creamy drinks as they leisurely strolled the boardwalk that Josh said, "So where did you and your folks go when you left Elk Creek?"

Megan stopped mid-sip to look at him out of the corner of her eye. "Aren't you ready to go off-duty yet?"

"I am *off-duty*. That was a purely friendly question."

"Honestly?"

"Honestly."

"Or at least it was a purely friendly question unless I just happen to say something that could be used against my parents."

"Okay, we don't have to talk. I was just making con-versation. Trying to get to know you a little."

"Without any ulterior motive?"

He rolled his eyes and shook his head. "Without any ulterior motive."

Megan didn't say anything for a while, weigh-ing whether he was telling her the truth or if he was fishing under the guise of friendliness and conversation-making.

She couldn't be sure. But on the other hand, she also couldn't think of anything she might say in answer to his question about where her family had gone after leaving Elk Creek that could be used against her folks, either.

So she finally said, "From here we went to California to work on improving the conditions of migrant laborers. We were there until after the first of the next year."

"And then?"

"And then," she repeated as if it were hardly that simple. "And then it isn't easy to remember it all in chronological order. For a while after California we were on a ship in the Bering Sea. But after that? There were picket lines and protests and petitions against fast-burning plutonium reactors, oil spills, toxic landfills, refrigeration units leaking hydro-fluorocarbons, petroleum derivatives seeping into the water basins, and forgotten nerve-gas bomblettes found near suburban developments. We spent time in the Arctic Circle. We went to Russia after Chernobyl. Basically, you name the site of an environmental hazard or a human or animal travesty and that's where I've been."

"You're well-traveled, is that what you're telling me?" he understated.

"More or less," Megan confirmed with a laugh.

"Wouldn't it have been simpler for your parents to do something more mainstream that still aimed for the same goals? Like going to work for the EPA, for instance?"

"Now you're talking about forcing them into a mold.

That has never worked for my folks. Or for Nissa or I, either," she added pointedly.

"Have you ever tried?"

Again she gave him a sideways glance, this one even more suspicious and leery than the last. "We're interested in *effecting* change, not in being changed ourselves."

"Okay," he said as if he knew when he was up against a brick wall. "What about school then? You left here after the sixth grade. You had to get farther than that. Or was formal education too *molding,* too?"

"Mostly my folks taught us. Occasionally they'd enroll us in a school for a few months if they thought we were going to be in one place that long. But more often they played teacher and then we'd have to take equivalency tests to get credit for having finished a grade. Of course the curriculum on the bus was a lot heavier on the civics and social sciences side than when we were in real schools, but Nissa and I both got our diplomas and scored high enough on the SATs to have our choice of colleges."

"You went to college?"

Megan turned her head to look straight at him that time. "Don't sound so amazed. I have a degree in biochemistry and Nissa has one in biology. We were both accepted into medical school but decided not to go the traditional route."

Josh smiled sheepishly. "It wasn't that I was doubting your intelligence. It just didn't sound like you'd ever stayed in one place long enough for higher education."

"Nissa and I did. Well, for the two and a half years it

took us to get our degrees. Our folks spent most of that time in the rain forest."

"And then you graduated and went back on the road?"

"Surprised again? Yes, we went back on the road. Our folks aren't the only ones who believe that it's important to stand up to the wrongdoers of the world. After college I went on to learn acupuncture and Nissa went into massage and herbal medicine and when we completed all that training we went back to the traveling lifestyle, practicing wherever we were at any given time at Peoples' fairs, Renaissance festivals, or just from the motor home."

"And then you decided to come to Elk Creek?" he said as if it didn't seem to fit.

Megan laughed again. "I know. We aren't going to find many wrongdoers to stand up to around here—especially since even though Nissa and I are vegetarians we aren't as militant about it as our folks are. But the thing is, my sister and I just got really, really tired of living like nomads. We started craving a more normal life. A chance to make friends and have families of our own. To put down roots. Maybe it's latent rebellion against our parents," she added with a joke.

"And *then* you thought of Elk Creek," Josh surmised.

"It was the only place either of us had ever actually considered home. Certainly it was the place we'd lived the longest in our lives. And there was the house my grandparents had built. A little bit of land. We just decided, hey, what better place?"

They'd reached her office by then and Megan let them in the front door, turning on the lights as she did.

"Elk Creek *is* a pretty good place," Josh agreed, coming in with her.

"Mmm. After today I'm beginning to wonder," she muttered, more to herself than to him.

"Don't hold today against the whole town. For one, it wasn't the whole town. And for two, this is an odd situation and no matter where you are, in an odd situation, people tend to think the worst and come out of the woodwork with bizarre theories—it was one of the lessons of sheriff's training."

"But still Nissa and I are faced with having to convince them all—and you—that our parents didn't have anything to do with that backyard burial, then drum up interest and belief in the benefits of acupuncture, massage and herbal therapy, before we can actually make a living and have a life here—that's slightly more than we bargained for when we made this decision."

"Is the eternal optimist hitting a bump in the road?" he cajoled with a kindness that was new. And very sweet.

"Who said I'm an eternal optimist?"

Josh shrugged one of those broad shoulders. "I'm just guessing. But don't you have to be to believe you can take on the wrongdoers of the world and make them do right?"

"Maybe. I hadn't thought about it like that."

"It'll all work out," he assured her.

"It'll all work out?" she repeated with a wry laugh. "But only if you discover what really happened eighteen years ago and that my family had nothing to do with it."

"Which is what you're watch-doggin' me to make sure of."

"Yes, I am."

It must have been the return of a certain amount of bravado in her tone that made him chuckle. But it was a nice sound in the quiet of the office.

Then he said, "Maybe tomorrow we can get out and do what we were supposed to do today—talk to your neighbors. You can keep your fingers crossed that something more conclusive will turn up and lead us in a different direction."

"And what about your acupuncture? Shall we try to do that tomorrow, too?"

He made the face she was coming to think of as his acupuncture face.

"Not tomorrow. If I even come into town we're liable to be stuck here again. I'll just pick you up at your place."

"So still no acupuncture."

"I'll get around to it," he said without much conviction.

"We could do it right now," she suggested just to see him squirm.

He didn't squirm, though. He just bathed her in the warm brilliance of a thousand-watt grin. "Can't do it now. I need to get home, get to bed. Good police work takes a rested cop."

"Um-hmm," she said to let him know she saw through him.

Josh finished his hot chocolate then and tossed the paper cup into the trash basket beside her desk.

It seemed like a signal that he was wrapping things up and Megan couldn't think of any reason to delay that—despite the fact that she tried—so she dropped her own empty cup in the trash, too.

That left the matter of his coat, which she was still wearing.

She knew she needed to give it back to him but she wasn't eager to do that, either. She was enjoying having it around her. Too much, she knew.

So, with one last deep, indulging breath of the aftershave scent that infused it, Megan shrugged out of the jacket and handed it to him. "Thanks for that, anyway."

"Sure." Josh put it on and smiled. "Thanks for warming it up."

There was nothing about that that should have titillated her, but somehow it did. The titillation, though, was just one more thing she fought.

"Do you want me to drive you back to the courthouse?" she asked then, hating the breathy undertone her voice had taken without warning. Or good reason.

"It's tempting but I think I need a little more air. Is your car out back?"

"In the alley."

Josh nodded.

It was a simple, courteous, meaningless exchange. But something between them seemed to change suddenly. It seemed to slow down. To turn intimate.

"What time tomorrow?" Megan asked, trying to

combat that sense of intimacy along with everything else she was working against.

"Better make it ten. We don't want folks answering their doors in their pajamas."

"And you won't do anything without me before that?"

"Not anything that has to do with this case. I don't want to be pegged as one of the wrongdoers you need to avenge."

Megan smiled at his teasing, wishing that she didn't like him so much. Knowing only too well that she *shouldn't* like him so much.

But it didn't make any difference because she couldn't stop it.

Any more than she could stop those thoughts about a good-night kiss from creeping into her mind. Again.

On guard, she reminded herself once more. *Be on guard against it.*

But the warning didn't help any more than wishing she didn't like him so much had.

Because there they were, standing just a few feet inside the door, face to face, and Megan was looking up into midnight-blue eyes that seemed to emit enough heat to melt steel. Certainly enough to melt her and all her resolves.

Then, without warning, Josh leaned in and actually did kiss her. Barely. A simple peck on the lips. An impulse cut short when he realized what he'd done.

The expression on his face—still so close above hers—mirrored her surprise even as he grinned again.

A lopsided grin. "Whoops," he said as if the kiss had been an accident.

"Slipped and fell, did you?"

"I think I did. Internally, anyhow. Guess I'll have to watch my step in the future."

"Guess so," Megan confirmed to hide that she was really wishing he'd kiss her again. Longer this time…

But he didn't. Instead he took two steps backward and opened the office door.

"See you in the morning," he said in a husky voice, his gaze staying on her as if it were glued there.

"In the morning," Megan repeated, watching him go outside.

As he did he shook his head and said, "Oh, man," to himself.

Megan wasn't sure what that meant but it was the last thing he said before closing the door and heading back up the street the way they'd come.

It wasn't his reaction to that kiss that disturbed her, though. It was the fact that she had been so out of bounds.

What am I doing? she wondered even as she followed his same path to the door and watched him through the glass.

The guy had, just moments before, talked about changing her. About fitting into molds. Wasn't that enough of an indication of how much he was like Noel to turn her off? she demanded of herself.

Apparently not since she was now craning to keep sight of him.

And that sight of him—tall and lean and muscular,

with only the hint of a swagger to his gait—was a big part of her downfall and she knew it. He was just *too* good-looking. *Too* charming. *Too* sexy.

And she was *too* susceptible to it all.

Which was why she was supposed to have kept up her guard.

Disgusted with herself, Megan left the window, turning off the lights as she did. Then she went out the back door, into the alley and got into her cold car.

But that chill was just what she needed, she thought. It was like a cold shower to chase away desire.

And maybe the reason Josh had wanted to walk back to the courthouse….

But she didn't even want to entertain the idea that he might be experiencing what she was experiencing. Something about that made the whole situation seem all the more dangerous.

She started the engine and put the car into gear, driving slowly out of the alley and turning onto Center Street to go home.

Unfortunately Josh couldn't walk as fast as she could drive and within moments she was gaining on him.

Speed up! she ordered herself. *Get past him as quick as you can!*

But, on its own, her foot went to the brake instead, slowing her down.

She barely managed to refrain from stopping completely and asking him again if he wanted a ride. But despite that, despite the fact that she succeeded in resisting the urge to have just a few more minutes with him, it didn't change the fact that she wanted those few more minutes with him.

A few more minutes with him that might give her the chance for just one more kiss....

Chapter 5

MEGAN'S TEN O'CLOCK DATE with Josh to interview her neighbors didn't come about. First he called to say he couldn't make it at ten because he'd had a call from the head of the Sheriff's department and had to meet with him to update him on the case, that they would have to postpone their plans until the afternoon. Then he called at two to say the forensics report was in and he had to go over it with the medical examiner, that he still intended to talk to her neighbors today but that it wouldn't be until later. Megan had assured him she was available whenever he was ready.

The delays were good, she decided along the way. They gave her extra time to shore up her defenses against Josh's appeal.

The delays also gave her time to wash her hair and twirl it up into a spiky topknot that she held in place with tiny clips. They gave her time to give herself a manicure. To press her ankle-length, flowing flowered skirt and the two T-shirts she wore with it. The delays even gave her time to try on beaded necklaces until she found just the right combination in three that picked up the burnished red, cocoa brown, and autumn gold of her skirt.

But at four-thirty when Josh pulled up in front of her house and got out of his patrol car as she watched for him through the living room window, her whole day's worth of shoring up her defenses weakened.

Somehow, when he wasn't right there in front of her, she forgot just how great-looking he was—all tall and muscular and broad-shouldered. She forgot just how powerfully handsome were those features carved in perfect sharp angles and planes. How striking were his deep, dark-blue eyes. How intriguing those lips that had kissed her the night before...

Josh's knock on the front door helped break her reverie and Megan took a deep breath as she went to answer it, trying to re-shore her crumbling defenses.

She didn't exhale until she had the door open and then she forced a nervous smile, hoping she could—for once—rise above the things he churned up in her with just a single glimpse of him.

"Hi," she greeted as she pushed on the screen door to invite him inside.

"I'm sorry for this," he answered as he stepped across the threshold, sounding harried. "I didn't mean to keep you hanging all day."

"It's okay. I understand. And since I didn't have any acupuncture scheduled anyway, it was no big deal. I got some things taken care of around here."

Ha! That was a joke. All she'd done was get herself ready to see him again.

But she didn't want to think about that.

Josh went into the center of the room but he didn't sit down. He seemed too agitated, too preoccupied, to relax. Instead he just turned to Megan, his brow slightly furrowed.

"I don't suppose you've heard from your parents yet, have you?" he asked then, still skipping any amenities.

"No, I haven't," Megan answered, indulging in the scent of aftershave that had come in with him. But she realized even as she did that it wasn't helping her defenses any and wished he was wearing something that made him smell like swamp gas so it would turn her off rather than on.

"I'm taking some heat for not having at least spoken to my prime suspects," he admitted, confirming that he had a lot on his mind.

"There's nothing you or anyone else can do about it."

"That doesn't seem to matter."

Megan moved away from the front door and hung onto the back of a rocking chair her father had handcrafted, hoping to ground herself from the potency of Josh's effects on her.

"What about the forensics report?" she asked, going with the flow of the conversation Josh seemed intent on pursuing. "Did that tell you something that's making it more urgent that you talk to my folks?"

"If you mean did forensics turn up something that made it look worse for them, no. The bones were studied and X-rayed but there weren't any telltale signs. No breaks, no knife-nicks, nothing that looked as if it had been grazed by a bullet, all the neck bones were intact and so was the skull. And there wasn't a bullet recovered from the site or any bullet holes or knife gashes in the clothes," he said as if reciting a speech. "The bottom line is that they're reasonably sure he wasn't stabbed or shot, and that the cause of death wasn't a blow to the head, so there's still no telling how he died."

"And for sure it's the skeleton of a man?"

"No doubt about it. Plus forensics went through the pockets of the clothes and the knapsack. The man's name was Pete Chaney—it was on a bottle of nitro-glycerin tablets and on a Nebraska driver's license that expired five years before he did. Does the name ring any bells?"

Megan thought about it, then shook her head. "Not with me. But did you say he had nitroglycerin tablets? Doesn't that mean he had a heart problem? Maybe that's how he died—from a heart attack. And if that's true then there's no crime here at all."

"There's still the issue of not reporting a death to the authorities and the unlawful disposal of human remains," Josh pointed out.

"Maybe it was his last wish."

Josh didn't look convinced. "You think his last wish was to be buried on the sly in a shallow grave in someone's backyard?"

Okay, when he put it that way it didn't sound too likely.

"Besides, just because there isn't any evidence of a knife or a gun or a baseball bat doesn't mean he died of natural causes. He could still have been poisoned, strangled or suffocated—none of those would show up in what we were left with."

"But what's *not* there can't count against my folks."

"And speaking of what's not there," Josh said as if she'd just played right into his hand. "If Pete Chaney was the drifter old Buzz was talking about yesterday, and he had valuable coins of some kind, where are they? They weren't with his remains."

"Which is making you think what?" Megan probed since that seemed to be important to him.

"I'm just wondering where your folks got the money to move without selling their property. And where they got the money to go on following their causes from one place to another."

"Oh, so now my parents are not only murderers, they're thieves, too?"

"Just asking."

Megan stared at Josh for a long moment, trying to use the annoyance about his suspicions to counteract the other effects he was having on her. Like the fact that she was ultra-aware of the line of his jaw where today's uniform shirt brushed it. Like the way a slight smattering of hair curled up tantalizingly beneath his open collar. Like the way the shirt barely contained his pectorals and then billowed more loosely at the waist where it was tucked into jeans that fit him so well they could have been hand-tailored for him. Like the bulge of thick thighs…and other things…within the confines of those jeans…

Megan realized suddenly that she'd lost track of

what they'd been talking about. Certainly it hadn't had anything to do with what a terrific body he had.

She fought for recollection. There was a question in the air, she remembered that much. What was it? Ah, how her parents had financed themselves when they'd left Elk Creek…

"My folks never had much cash to speak of. They worked odd jobs along the way, devoting themselves to their causes once the bills were paid. I don't know why they didn't sell the farm but I'm sure it wasn't because the new owner might have dug up the body they'd buried in the backyard," she said facetiously. "It's a much better bet that they hung onto the place because it's all they actually owned and it's been in the family for so long they didn't want to part with it. But when I talk to them I'll ask."

"When you talk to them you'd better just tell them to get hold of me and I'll ask."

Megan reared back at the force of his command. "Wow, you must have had a tough day," she said.

Josh screwed up his face. "Sorry. Yes, I did have a bad day. Everybody wants this thing solved but they tie me up with one harebrained story after another. And now I have a superior who doesn't stop to think that every hour I spend explaining to him why I haven't gotten further in this investigation is causing me not to get further in this investigation."

Frustration echoed in his voice but he shook his head, as if he were trying to shake it off.

"Don't mind me. I'm just in the eye of the storm," he said then. "How about if I disappear into your kitchen, wash my hands, have a drink of water, and get rid of this lousy mood I'm in before I come out again?"

"Sounds like a plan," Megan agreed.

"Great. Give me five minutes and I promise I'll be a new man."

Megan nodded, thinking that even if he was in a foul mood she didn't want a new man.

Not that she *wanted* Josh, she was quick to amend in her own mind as she watched him head for the other room.

The five minutes he was out of her sight seemed like forever. But then Josh returned with a sheepish grin on his face, looking surprisingly refreshed.

"Well, hi, Ms. Bailey," he said, pretending to start over. "You're a sight for sore eyes if ever there was one. How're you doin' today?"

Megan laughed. "Better than you are."

"Me? Why, I'm doin' just fine now that I'm with you."

She thought he was teasing her, especially with those g's he didn't usually drop from the end of his words unless he was trying to be charming. But she couldn't help a flicker of hope that he might mean what he was saying. Just a little.

"Neighbors," she said to remind him why he was really there before that flicker was fanned into a flame.

"Neighbor," he countered, not seeming to have any problem getting back to the business at hand. "Thinking about it last night in bed I realized we talked to all but two of the folks closest to you yesterday. And of those two, the Jagsons, didn't buy their land until ten years ago, so they weren't around when this guy disappeared. That only leaves Mabel Murphy to the south for us to talk to."

It was disheartening to hear that last night, when Megan had been lying in bed reliving that kiss he'd planted on her just before leaving, he'd been lying in his bed thinking about this case. But she tried not to get too stuck on that and concentrated on the rest of what he'd said.

"I remember the Murphys," she informed him. "They seemed like grandparents when I lived here before. They must be as old as dirt by now."

"Horace died a while back, but Mabel still gets around. And her mind is sharp. I called to let her know we'd be coming. Unfortunately I've kept her waiting all day, too."

"Then we shouldn't keep her waiting anymore, should we?"

"No, I guess we shouldn't."

Was she mistaken or did he sound reluctant to get on their way?

"Don't you want to go?"

"It's not that. I've just had another long day already and I'm feeling the urge to play hooky with a pretty girl. I'll get over it. Come on."

Megan wasn't altogether certain that she was the *pretty girl* he was referring to but the offhand comment still managed to re-light that flicker in her.

Up and down again. Why was it that she couldn't be with him without riding an emotional teeter-totter?

But Megan didn't have an answer for that as she followed Josh's lead to the front door he held open for her. He repeated the courtesy at the passenger side of his patrol car, then got behind the wheel himself.

"So you still didn't tell me how old Mabel Murphy is," Megan said as they headed for the main road.

"Ninety-three, I believe."

"And she lives on her own?"

"Sturdy stock is what she attributes it to. The farm has all gone fallow now, she can't work it of course. But she seems to do a pretty good job of taking care of herself."

The Murphy place was Megan's nearest neighbor so that was about all the time they had for conversation before Josh pulled up in front of a farmhouse similar to Megan's. The white paint was peeling here and there, but otherwise it was in better repair than hers.

The front door opened as Megan and Josh got out of the car, telling them that Mabel had been watching for them the same way Megan had been watching for Josh just shortly before.

"Is that you, Megan?" a strong voice called from the doorway.

Apparently Josh had told her he wasn't coming alone.

"It's me," Megan confirmed, preceding Josh up the porch steps to the door.

Mabel Murphy seemed to have shrunk since the last time Megan had seen her. She'd never been a large woman but now she was so tiny and so frail that, even at barely five feet four inches herself, Megan towered over her.

"Oh, let me get a good look at you," the elderly woman ordered once Megan and Josh were in the entryway with the door closed behind them. "Didn't you grow up to be beautiful!"

Megan thanked her for the compliment, taking in her neighbor's sparse, cottony white hair curled into a round bubble and the tissuey skin of her map-lined face. But Mabel's brown eyes were still sparkling with life in spite of it all and that was what made Megan say, "You're looking good."

Mabel flapped a fragile hand in the air to shoo away the very thought. Then she said, "I hope you still like pot roast, Josh. And, Megan, if memory serves, you loved my potato patties and the snickerdoodles I made for dessert," she ended in a whisper, as if Megan's parents might be lurking around the corner to forbid her the sweets.

Megan shot Josh a glance that said *I didn't know we were eating here.*

But apparently neither did he because from behind the elderly woman he shrugged elaborately and held both hands out—palms upward—to relay that this was news to him, too.

Then he said, "I didn't mean for you to cook for us, Mabel. If I hadn't been held up we would have been here this morning."

"Oh I know, I know. But after your second phone call to let me know you wouldn't be here until late afternoon

I thought, *gotcha! Now I can rope 'em into stayin' to eat with an old woman.*"

They all laughed at her candor.

Then she added, "Unless you can't and then don't worry about it. I'll just have leftovers."

But it was clear she was lonely and eager for the company.

Josh must have seen it, too, because he was quick to say, "I know I don't have any other plans. If Megan does I can take her home and come back."

Megan liked him all the more for that and for not so much as hesitating to accept the invitation as if it pleased him no end. But she tried not to let it show.

"I can stay, too," she informed them. "As long as you're sure it's no trouble."

Mabel waved away that notion, too. "Let's go into the kitchen and have a glass of wine while I get things ready. You know, they're saying wine's good for you now. But I've known it all along. It's what got me where I am today. And don't go tellin' me you're on duty, Josh. Dinner time means work's done."

Except that it was barely dinner time by anyone's standards. But he didn't point that out. He merely said, "Yes, ma'am," and winked at Megan over the other woman's head.

Mabel led them down a hall that ran beside the staircase but she stopped short a few feet from the archway that connected the kitchen up ahead.

"Remember this, Megan?" she asked, pointing to an old-fashioned, seated hall-tree built like a wooden throne with an etched, oval mirror in the upper half, ornate hooks on either side of it, and arms that were curved into loops that held umbrellas in one and antique walking sticks in the other.

"I do remember it," Megan admitted. "My dad made it for you."

"Fine craftsman, your dad." Mabel bent over and raised the lid on the seat. "Even has a little hiding place here. It's where I keep the love letters my Horace sent me when I was a girl," she confided as if it were a great secret.

Then she set the lid back down and adjusted the needlepoint cushion on it. "Is your dad still doing wood-work like this?"

"Not a lot. He left all his big tools here when we left and we were never in one place long enough for him to start up another workshop."

"That's a shame," Mabel said as they went the rest of the way down the hall to the kitchen.

Once they were there the smells of pot roast and potatoes greeted them as Mabel poured three jelly glasses full of wine and ordered Megan and Josh to sit at the already set table while she sliced the meat.

It wasn't until they were eating—Megan quietly bypassing the meat and dining on salad, potatoes and bread—that Mabel's questions about Megan's family dwindled. When they did she angled a glance toward Josh.

"So you have some things you want to ask me, do you?" the elderly woman said straight out.

"Great meal," Josh complimented rather than immediately answering, pointing his fork at his plate and sounding as if he'd never tasted anything so good.

Then he took another bite of the succulent roast, chewed and swallowed and made a contented cat face before he finally explained the discovery in Megan's backyard.

"A *skeleton,* did you say? Just next door?"

"Don't get alarmed," Josh was quick to tell her. "This isn't something that just happened. It's been there for the past eighteen years. We're thinking the man's name was Pete Chaney, that he might have been a drifter who passed through here."

"A drifter named Pete Chaney," Mabel repeated, obviously thinking about it.

"I need to know if you recognize the name or if you remember anything about someone who might have been around then. Anything at all."

"There've been a lot of drifters through Elk Creek over the years. Farm hands. Ranch hands. And eighteen years ago is a long time."

"Buzz Martindale thought he recalled somebody being around about then who bragged that he owned some kind of valuable coins. Does that help?"

Mabel scratched her wattled neck with one arthritic finger. "What kind of coins?"

"I don't know. That's all Buzz remembered—the rumor of them. He never saw them and they didn't turn up with the rest of Pete Chaney's things. I called Buzz again today with the name of the man. He said it was vaguely familiar but he couldn't even be sure if that was the name that went with the coin story."

After another moment of what appeared to be Mabel scanning her memory, she finally shook her head. "I'm sorry, Josh. I thought my brain cells were in better shape than the rest of me, but I'm drawing a blank. But then you can't really go by me too much. I never had a lot of contact with anybody just passing through. Even when we hired a stranger to work here it was only for a day or two and Horace dealt with them, I didn't. He kept them away from me and the house just in case they were up to no good somehow, so I never really got to know any of them."

"What about somebody around the Bailey place next door? Do you remember anything about Megan's family having someone around just before they left town? Maybe he was one of the people they took in or a friend or relative?"

"The Baileys were always taking in *somebody*." Mabel cast an apologetic glance at Megan and then added, "Horace and I thought the world of the Baileys themselves, but Horace was as leery of those folks they'd take in as he was of any strangers he had to hire around here. He always had me keep my distance from them, too. The strangers, I mean, not the Baileys. So I never got to know who was over there, either." Mabel made it sound as if she might have liked to.

Then she shrugged a bony shoulder and said, "I'm not being much help, am I?"

"That's all right," Josh assured her. "Just keep thinking about it. Maybe something will come to you later on. A comment Horace might have made. Something."

"I'll do that. I'll even go through Horace's old papers,

see if I can find that Pete Chaney name in any of it. Maybe there'll be some kind of clue there."

The elderly woman seemed intrigued by the mystery now and it made both Josh and Megan smile.

"Every little bit helps, Miss Marple," Josh said, teasing her.

"Maybe you should make me your deputy," she joked in return.

From there conversation centered on people and events around town, finishing out the meal and taking them through cleanup—a chore Josh and Megan insisted on doing while Mabel had a cup of tea at the table.

Then, with a promise from Josh to come back for a game of gin rummy when he was out from under this case, he and Megan said good-night and left.

"Is pot roast and gin rummy with little old ladies in your job description?" Megan asked as Josh drove away from the Murphy place.

"Perks, those are the perks," he said as if he meant it.

"It's nice of you."

"It's no big deal," he demurred gruffly, obviously uncomfortable with the praise. "I'd rather do that than have my only contact with people be writing them traffic tickets or arresting them."

"I thought cops *liked* to give traffic tickets and arrest people," she joked to give him a hard time.

"Not this cop," he said with a hard stare out of the corner of his eye.

"Is that why you don't wear a gun? So you can be the friendly cop rather than the intimidating cop?"

"That and that I don't really have a need for one most of the time."

"Why *did* you want to be sheriff?" Megan asked, drinking in the sight of a profile so striking it could have adorned Roman coins.

"There were financial reasons, for one. You know my family's spread is not the biggest in the county. All but Devon work the place—"

"What does Devon do?"

"He became a veterinarian and stayed away."

"Ah. Sorry to interrupt. Go on with what you were saying."

"I was saying that the rest of my brothers and I work the ranch but we all do other things to supplement the income and to save so we can expand. When the sheriff's job opened up I thought, *why don't I do that?* It's full-time pay but hardly full-time work hours."

"You've seemed to put in full-time work hours since I met you."

"Sure, but when I'm not tracking down eighteen-year-old crimes I generally have at least part of every day free to work the ranch. As long as I keep my pager and my cellular phone handy so Millie can reach me if the need arises there's no reason for me to be in town all the time."

"Okay, so you wanted to be sheriff for the money and short hours. But that was only for starters. Why else did you want to do it?" she prompted.

"I like being involved, helping out, really participating in the community and making a difference. Protecting and serving—if that doesn't sound too hokey. I know from the activist tree-hugger perspective I'm *the Man* and that's a bad thing, but around here that's not how I'm looked at," he said, getting in a jab of his own.

He was right, though. Frequently her parents referred to the police in the negative and viewed them as champions of the environmental offenders who hauled the protestors off to jail for the smallest infraction.

But Megan didn't want to confirm Josh's presumption of what her family thought of law enforcement so she didn't say anything at all.

She didn't fool Josh, though. When the short drive from Mabel's house came to an end and he pulled up in front of Megan's house, he turned off the engine, swiveled in his seat so he was angled in her direction and said, "I hit the nail on the head, didn't I? I'm the big, bad Man."

He was a big man all right, but Megan had difficulty seeing anything bad in him.

Not that she'd let him know that.

"Any protests or demonstrations that I've ever been a part of were peaceful and orderly. But I have had occasion to think that the cops watching us with an eagle eye instead of going after the real offenders were on the wrong side."

"Um-hmm. Well, here I'm generally considered to be on the *right* side. Nobody wants cars speeding through town or shopkeepers ripped off or homes broken into or—"

"Or bodies buried in the backyard," she added for him.

"Or bodies buried in the backyard. And I'm here to take care of it if it does happen."

"Along with eating pot roast and playing gin rummy with little old ladies," Megan repeated. "I still think that's above and beyond the call of duty and nice of you."

And he was no more comfortable with the comment now than he had been a few moments earlier.

"Mabel's a good ol' girl," was his only response.

"And you're a good man," Megan said, realizing in that instant how true it was. She'd been raised with a be-kind-to-everyone-and-everything philosophy and it wasn't always easy to find that attitude in other people. She appreciated it when she did. And she was pretty sure she just had. In Josh.

But still he looked skeptical of her opinion of him. "Tell me what a good guy I am if it turns out I have to arrest your parents."

"You won't," Megan responded confidently. "They didn't do anything."

Josh didn't argue the point. He just arched a brow at her.

Then he said, "I will give you a heads-up, though, if you're interested."

"I am."

"I have orders to interview your folks ASAP no matter what. That means if you don't get through to them to tell them to call me for a phone interview within the next twenty-four hours I'm to set the wheels into motion for Peruvian officials to take them off that ship you say they're on and turn them over for extradition."

Megan rolled her eyes at that, unfazed by the threat. "I can put in another call but it won't change anything. They still have to be contacted and then arrange to get back to me. And even if that takes longer than the next twenty-four hours they're still bound to do that before you make it all the way through channels and red tape to have them extradited just for questioning. It's a waste of your time."

"My superior doesn't think so," Josh said, his tone letting her know he agreed with her rather than with the higher-up. "Look, just between you and me, I wouldn't be threatening extradition until I was one hundred percent sure I had a murder on my hands here. But like I said, I have orders. So do me a favor and spend tomorrow trying to get hold of your parents again."

"You don't have to follow the orders, you know."

"Are you trying to incite insubordination?" he asked as if she amused him.

"How'm I doing?"

"You're failing miserably."

"Even with all my charms at full force?" she joked.

"Even with all your charms at full force," he confirmed, but his smile and the heat coming from his eyes let her know he didn't take her charms lightly.

It occurred to Megan then that they were still sitting in his car, that she should either invite him in or say good-night.

Of course she knew which of those she *should* do. But even so, she heard herself say, "Would you like to come in?"

His gaze went from her to the house and back again as if he were tempted.

But then he said, "I don't think so. I'd better slip into my office while I can do it without drawing any attention and see if there's anything I should take care of other than this case. I'll walk you to the door, though."

"You don't have to do that," she said in a hurry, thinking that fate was offering her a reprieve from her own misdirected inclinations and that she should take it.

But it didn't matter because Josh opened his car door and got out as he said, "I want to."

Megan didn't wait for him to come around to her side of the car. She got out on her own and headed for her front porch with Josh trailing behind her.

"What will you be doing tomorrow while I'm trying to reach my parents again?" she asked then.

"Why, will you miss me?" he teased.

"No, I'm watch-dogging you to make sure you pay close enough attention to other leads, remember?"

"I remembered, I was just hoping for more," he said, feigning disappointment that she hadn't played along. But since she hadn't he conceded and answered her question about what he would be doing the next day. "My full agenda is to review and organize all the notes I took during yesterday's interviews to make sure I didn't overlook anything. I'll be calling the people who actually made some sense to ask if they remember the name Pete Chaney. Plus I'm going to make copies of everything to give to my superior just to let him see that I'm as much on top of this as I can be. And I'm doing it all from home to avoid being distracted by drop-ins at the office. You won't be missing anything."

Except being with him.

But she didn't say that either. She knew she shouldn't have even thought it.

They'd reached her front door by then but neither of them made a move to open it. Instead they stood in the dim glow of the porch light, face to face, and only separated by a scant foot of empty space.

"Just concentrate on getting through to your parents and don't worry about watch-dogging me for a day," Josh said in conclusion.

His voice was more quiet all of a sudden and there was something about it, something about the way he was looking at her, that made Megan feel as though his eyes were holding hers, that made thinking coherently seem like a struggle.

Well, not thinking about everything. It wasn't a struggle to think about him. To revel in the sight of broad shoulders and a face as handsome as any she'd ever seen. To wonder if he might kiss her again. To want him to so much it was like a desert thirst...

But kissing was a bad idea and she knew it. She really did. She knew it.

Yet still her gaze slipped from Josh's midnight-blue eyes down his straight, thin nose to those lips that had touched hers so briefly the night before and the thirst only grew stronger to feel them pressed to hers again.

And then he leaned slightly forward, pulled away and leaned forward once more—all without actually coming close enough to kiss her but obviously with that intent, allowing her the opportunity to escape before he did, if she was so inclined.

But the only thing she was inclined to do was stay where she was to have him kiss her. Bad idea or not. So she tipped her chin up just a fraction of an inch to let him know she was willing. Hoping it didn't seem eager even though that's just what she was.

Josh read the signal. He leaned the rest of the way in and did kiss her.

Not so short this time, she mentally beseeched, worrying that it might be just another hit-and-run kiss like the one from the previous evening.

But it wasn't just another hit-and-run kiss. This time he stayed long enough for her to actually experience the gentleness of his mouth against hers.

To experience it and savor it.

His lips were smooth, parted just so. He knew the exact moment to deepen the kiss, to move in a sexy little circle that was enticing enough to draw her to her toes for more.

He tasted spicy, probably from the snickerdoodles Mabel had served for dessert, and his breath on her cheek was deliciously warm.

Megan loved the scent of his aftershave and she began to feel swept away by that kiss, wonderfully disconnected from everything but Josh, from the investigation and the suspicions of her parents, from the whole rest of the world.

The only things missing were his arms around her or the touch of his hands, the chance to be up against him, her straining breasts melding with those impressive pectorals of his.

But not only didn't she get any of that, about the time she was thinking about it, craving it the most, Josh ended the kiss. And even though it was more than the hit-and-run kiss of the previous evening, it was still over before she wanted it to be.

But at least tonight he didn't act as if it were out of his control. Tonight, when he stopped kissing her, he went back to looking into her eyes, to bathing her in that hot honey gaze as if he were committing her face to memory.

"I'll talk to you tomorrow," he said then.

Megan could only nod as she fought to regain herself, to bounce back from that kiss when what she really wanted to do was melt into his arms so he could kiss her again. So he could go on kissing her all night long. Or until she'd had her fill.

If she could ever *get* her fill...

But then he just said good-night and returned to his patrol car, leaving her there to watch him go and bite her tongue to keep from begging him to stay.

He waved one big hand at her before he ducked into the driver's seat, restarted the engine and pulled away, but only after his taillights nearly disappeared into the distance did Megan realize she hadn't answered his wave with one of her own.

She'd just stood there, watching him. Wanting him. Too weak from that kiss, too lost in its lingering effects, to do anything but stand there in a daze. A daze of longing for more.

But then she yanked herself back to reality and finally turned to go inside.

And as she did she couldn't help wishing that things were different.

Until she reminded herself that that wish was why she couldn't make a go of any kind of personal relationship with Josh no matter how attracted she might be to him.

Because that wish that *things* were different led to the wish that *people* were different. It led to trying to change those people rather than accepting them the way they were.

And that, Megan knew better than anyone, was just a disaster waiting to happen.

Chapter 6

THE NEXT DAY WAS a red-letter day for Megan. It began with a call from a woman named Clair Winston for an appointment for an acupuncture treatment.

Nissa had met Clair at the Ladies' League dinner. Clair suffered from chronic back pain and while Nissa's massage therapy had helped somewhat, Clair had taken Nissa's recommendation that she see Megan for acupuncture.

"I was hoping you could fit me in today. I'm just so miserable," Clair said.

Megan smiled to herself and refrained from letting the woman know that she didn't have a single client yet, making the appointment for one that afternoon.

"Finally!" Megan rejoiced when she hung up, heading for her closet for good first-impression clothes.

She opted for a high-waisted denim dress that buttoned down the front, a pair of navy-blue tights and navy-blue clogs to go with them.

She pulled the sides of her hair to her crown and tied them in a knot, letting the ends spike off to one side. Then she pinched her cheeks, applied her henna mascara, and finished with multiple strands of beaded bracelets on both wrists.

Through it all Josh wasn't too far from her mind, though, and before she left for the office she put in another call to her parents, stressing that it was urgent that she speak to them. Speaking to them would give her an excuse to talk to Josh—and maybe see him— today. And while she told herself and told herself that that was unwise, that she should be looking for ways to avoid him—particularly after that kiss the previous evening and what it had done to her—she still couldn't help the bubble of hope that she wouldn't go a full day without contact with him.

With the message left for her parents, she forwarded her calls to the office phone and went there.

Clair Winston turned out to be a seventy-five-year-old woman with more bald spots than patches of hair. Megan spent nearly forty-five minutes talking with her about her back problems and a slew of other health issues she had, and then did the treatment.

The treatment turned out to be a good start for Megan because Clair felt so much better afterwards that she marveled at her own improvement and told Megan she couldn't wait to tell the girls in her bridge club. And a word-of-mouth endorsement was better than any amount of advertising.

When Clair left the office, Megan put in another call to her folks, thinking that when she spoke to them she could let them know that not only was Nissa getting business off the ground, but now so was she.

About four o'clock that afternoon those phone calls

finally paid off, too. Just as Megan was considering returning home the phone on her desk rang.

She knew the moment she picked up that it would be her parents on the other end because what she heard when she first held the receiver to her ear was so much static it sounded like someone crumpling tissue paper into the mouthpiece.

"Nissa? Is that you?" her father shouted from who-knew-where.

"No, Dad, it's Megan," she shouted in response.

"...bad connection...storm here...said it was an emergency..."

"We have a problem, Dad," Megan said, going on to explain as briefly—and as loudly—as she could what was going on.

"Pete Chaney?" her father repeated when she was finished. "...knew him. He was someone who just passed through town, looking for work."

The static suddenly stopped, leaving her father sounding as if he were talking to her from too much distance from a speaker phone. But at least she could hear every word now so he was easier to understand.

"So you did know Pete Chaney?" Megan asked for clarification now that none of his words were being lost.

"We hired him to help close up the farm. He worked during the day, when you girls were in school. He was a little odd and we didn't want him to be around you kids. But he was alive and well the last time I saw him."

"Could he have waited until we left town and then made himself at home in the house?"

"We offered to let him use the place after we were gone but he said he didn't want to. Said he didn't like to stay in one place too lo—"

A burst of static so loud it hurt Megan's ear caused her to flinch away from the phone. But it was gone when she held it to her ear once more.

Her father was in the middle of saying, "...quite a storyteller."

"Speaking of which, did he say anything about having some kind of valuable coins?"

"Two solid gold doubloons," her father confirmed. "He said he could sell them at any time and make himself a rich man. But I never saw them myself. I doubt they existed. Pete was a few cards short of a deck. He also claimed to remember the Spanish Inquisition from his own experience in a past life."

"But he was definitely alive and well when we left Elk Creek?"

"We passed him walking south on the main road as we were leaving. You girls thought he was a hobo."

Megan had no memory of that but it was hardly monumental enough to have stuck in her mind. Unfortunately. Maybe if it had it would help convince Josh of her parents' innocence.

More static assaulted Megan's hearing and this time even when it eased up enough to hear her father again it didn't disappear entirely. Once more she was only getting portions of what he said.

"...wasn't buried in the backyard, that's for sure."

"Dad, I have one more question and then I have to give you the name and number of the sheriff here. You need to get hold of him and let him interview you or they're talking about trying to have you and Mom taken off the ship and extradited."

"Extradited? That's a bunch of cra—"

"Dad? Dad? Are you there?"

The static was so bad that Megan had to hold the phone away from her ear again.

When she could bear to have it closer, she repeated, "Dad? Are you still there?"

"…try to call…when the storm's…"

And that was that.

The static was suddenly silenced and the call disconnected, and Megan was left without any reason to give Josh as to why her parents hadn't sold the farm when they'd left Elk Creek or where they'd gotten the money to begin their travels. Plus she hadn't given her father enough information to contact Josh, which Josh also wasn't going to be happy about.

But there wasn't anything else she could do.

Except stop by his house on her way home to tell him what little she *had* learned from the call.

If Megan had been asked to describe the Brimley house from memory she wouldn't have been able to. But once she had it in her sights she recognized it.

It was a two-story square clapboard box, the upper level the same size as the lower level. The roof helped distinguish it. It was steep and shingled in black, dropping eaves over three windows in the second story and echoed in a matching overhang below those windows to provide cover for a wrap-around porch.

A big old farmhouse was what it was. Nothing fancy, but well-kept with its white paint pristine and black shutters on either side of the front door and all the windows.

Megan particularly liked the homey touches in the twin carriage lamps that decorated the shutters that bracketed the front door, the planters that hung in the middle of each section of the cross-bucked railing that boarded the porch, and the spindled benches and high-backed rocking chairs just waiting for a cool breeze on a hot summer's evening.

As Megan pulled up in the circular drive where Josh's patrol car was parked, he came out the front door. But it was apparent that he hadn't heard or seen her approach because as he came down the porch steps his expression went from curious to surprised when he realized she was behind the wheel.

Then he paused for a bout of violent sneezing that didn't conclude until Megan had turned off the engine.

Or at least she thought the bout of sneezing had concluded. But he paused again two paces from the foot of the steps to sneeze several more times.

As he did Megan took in the sight of him. He wasn't dressed the way he had been any of the other times she'd seen him—in blue jeans and either a plain shirt or his uniform shirt. Instead he looked as if he were headed for an evening out. As if for a casual date.

He had on a nicer-than-usual pair of cowboy boots, black jeans and a crisp white shirt emblazoned with a red-and-black design that rode his broad shoulders like saddlebags and ended in points over each impressive pectoral. Plus he looked freshly showered and shaved— so freshly that his hair was still a tiny bit damp where the late-day, waning April sun glistened off it.

A date. A casual date. That initial thought replayed itself in Megan's mind. Could that be what he was about to embark on?

She hated how that idea made her feel. She hated it all the more because she knew it shouldn't bother her in the slightest.

But oh, did it bother her!

Who could he be going out with? she wondered. He hadn't mentioned that he was seeing someone. But then, why would he have? It wasn't as if they'd been dating themselves. Or even on a single date—regardless of how the evenings they'd spent together might have seemed.

But he *had* kissed her.

And what was he doing kissing her if he was involved with someone else?

Seeing someone else. *Dating* someone else. *Involved* with someone else. This was getting worse and worse in her mind with each passing moment. It was certainly making her feel worse and worse. But she couldn't help it.

Any more than she could help the sudden urge to restart her engine and just drive away. To force Josh to track her down to get the information he wanted from her. To make him work for it. If she gave it at all…

But even as she entertained the possibility, she knew she was being unreasonable. She didn't have any claim on him, kisses or no kisses. They weren't an item, let alone an exclusive item. And for all she knew, those kisses hadn't meant anything. They could just have been flukes. Spur-of-the-moment impulses. *Meaningless* spur-of-the-moment impulses...

That didn't help lift her spirits any and again she considered a fast getaway.

But then Josh got his sneezing under control and waved to her, and she knew she had to go through with this in spite of everything.

But why did he have to look so appealing as he came around his car and leaned his hips against the fender that faced her, waiting for her to join him? Why did every gesture have to be so sexy as he slipped his hands half-in, half-out of his pockets and stretched his long, thick legs into a lazy angle before he crossed them at the ankles?

And he was smiling, too. As if he were happy to see her. As if he didn't feel the tiniest hint of guilt for kissing her last night and dating someone else tonight.

Megan tried to steel herself and got out of her car, holding her head high and swearing she would not let him see how much this turn of events disturbed her.

"Hi," Josh greeted her, making it sound as if he were pleased that she was there.

"Hello," Megan answered coolly, aloofly, formally.

So coolly, aloofly and formally that it made Josh's brow wrinkle up in what appeared to be confusion.

"I didn't realize you might be on your way out. That you had plans," Megan added, her gaze dropping to his clothes and back to his achingly-handsome face again.

"I was on my way to look for you. That was my only plan," he said simply enough.

"All dressed up like that?" she demanded before she knew she was going to.

Josh glanced down at himself as if he wasn't sure what she was talking about. "Dressed like what?"

There was no way she was going to admit she'd thought he was dressed for a date so she said, "Out of uniform."

But it was feeble and they both knew it.

His greeting smile stretched into a grin and he said, "What did you think? That you'd just caught me headed for a hot night on the town with my harem?"

"Of course not," she said, trying to cover her tracks.

But he still saw through her.

"You did, didn't you? You thought I was on my way to see someone else of the female persuasion. And you didn't like it much." He chuckled to himself. "This is great. I love it."

Megan rolled her eyes, still trying for spin control. "Right. I couldn't stand the idea. I was green with envy."

"I think you were," he accused, laughing delightedly now.

"Think whatever you like," she said as if she were bored with the whole topic.

"I will."

Megan might have been more irritated by his pleasure except that it occurred to her then that not only had she been wrong about him going out on a date with someone else, but he'd decked himself out like that to go looking for her. And that helped soothe her ruffled feathers considerably.

"Is that why you came over here?" Josh asked then. "To check up on me?"

Megan finally managed to laugh and that went a lot further in sounding unperturbed than anything she'd attempted yet. "I came to tell you that I talked to my father, but if your ego is so huge that you want to think of me as your stalker, go ahead."

This time she must have convinced him because he said, "Sure, ruin all my fun." Then he gave in and got down to business. "So you talked to your father. How come I haven't?"

"Apparently there was a terrible storm wherever he was calling from because it was a really bad connection. I could barely hear him and just when I was about to give him your name and number we were cut off."

Josh held up one index finger as a sign for her to wait while he sneezed again. Twice.

"Gesundheit," Megan responded before going on. "I did find out a few things, but maybe we should go somewhere else to talk so you can concentrate."

"I'm concentrating just fine," he said, his tone laced with innuendo as his gaze remained intently on her. "Just tell me what your father had to say."

Megan repeated everything she'd learned from the phone call. Then she said, "I was all ready to ask your questions about why they didn't sell the house and where the traveling money came from when the call was disconnected. I did ask if my dad thought Chaney might have come back after we left, though. If maybe because he'd known the place would be empty he might have decided to set himself up for a little house-sitting. Dad didn't think Chaney would have done that because he and Mom offered to let Chaney stay there if he wanted to, but Chaney said he was ready to move on. What I'm wondering is if maybe Chaney changed his mind for some reason. Maybe he even opened up the house to another drifter—someone he knew. They could have had a fight, Chaney was killed, and the other drifter buried him and took off without anyone being the wiser."

"Were there signs that the house had been broken into or used when you opened it up again?"

"No, not really. There was a lot of dust on the dust-covers is about all. But still—"

"So you think not one, but two drifters set up house-keeping in your house without anyone knowing it? And while they were here they had a fight, one of them was killed and the other one buried him in the backyard? But there wasn't so much as a chair overturned in the process?"

"Maybe the second drifter cleaned up afterward so there *wouldn't* be a sign."

"Mmm. And how did this fight cause death without cracking the skull or any other bones?"

"Maybe he sat on Chaney and held a pillow over his face."

"And maybe pigs can fly, Megan. That's still not as likely as the possibility that your folks contributed to Chaney's demise to take his gold doubloons and bank-roll their escapades."

"Except that's not what happened. I told you, my father said he never saw the coins and he didn't think they existed."

"What else is he going to say if he took them and sold them?"

"Check coin dealers, why don't you? See if you find some place that bought gold doubloons from somebody. I'll bet you won't."

"As a matter of fact, hitting the coin dealers in Cheyenne is tomorrow's project."

"And I want to be there to say I-told-you-so when you find out no one has ever seen gold doubloons."

"I never doubted that you'd be right by my side," Josh said as if he were enjoying going head-to-head with her.

Then he had another sneezing attack before he said, "I still need to talk to your parents myself."

"I know. My father said he'd call back when the storm ends and I'll make sure the first thing I tell him is to get hold of you. But he isn't going to tell you anything different than he told me."

"Oh, okay, I'll just tell my superior I don't need to talk directly to my prime suspect because he told his daughter that he didn't do it."

Megan had a retort for that but before she could give it Josh went into more sneezing.

When it finally subsided, she said, "I can take care of that, you know."

"My superior? What are you proposing, Ms. Bailey?" he joked.

"Not a lap-dance for your boss," she said. "I can take

care of that allergy. Or at least I could if you weren't such a big baby about the needles."

"I'm not afraid of needles," he insisted, taking the bait.

"What are you afraid of, then? That acupuncture might work and I'll prove you wrong in that along with proving you wrong in suspecting my parents?"

Josh crossed his arms over his chest and smiled a smile that said he wasn't falling for any more of her tactics.

"I think you're just trying to get me on a table," he countered, his tone full of insinuation.

Okay, so that was an intriguing thought.

But she fought it.

"I had Clair Winston in today," Megan said instead, reminding herself that she was a professional. "By the time I was finished with her, she left a believer. But then I guess she's just more open-minded than you are."

"Is that so," he said noncommittally.

"You wouldn't have anything to lose. If I recall, our deal was that if it doesn't work, you don't pay."

"But I'd still have had needles stuck in me."

"You won't even feel them."

He went on staring at her and Megan didn't have any idea what was going through his mind.

But what was going through hers was that if he didn't agree to the acupuncture this brief encounter in his driveway would be the last they saw of each other today. That there wouldn't be any reason for him not to turn around and go back inside his house, or any reason for her not to go home to hers.

And as much as she knew that would be for the best, she hated the thought.

"Come on," she cajoled, hoping she wasn't being transparent. "If you don't have a hot date tonight what else do you have to do?"

The mention of a hot date made him smile again, the way he had when he'd believed—rightly—that she was jealous of that possibility.

But he didn't comment on it the way she thought he would. Instead he pushed off the fender with his hips—a motion that sent a little tingle of unexpected appreciation all through her—and opened the driver's side door on her car for her.

"Okay. I'll follow you to your torture chamber and be your pin cushion."

"Wise choice," Megan said as she worked to contain her pleasure and slid behind the wheel.

"Buckle up," he ordered.

"Yes, sir, officer, sir," she clipped out like a boot camp recruit.

But Josh merely smiled again, this time letting it stretch into a grin as he closed her door. Then he went to his own car.

Which left Megan watching the way those black jeans made his already to-die-for derriere look.

And thinking what an especially delicious delight the view was when it came with the knowledge that it wasn't the last she was going to get to see of him tonight.

Chapter 7

NISSA HAD ALREADY CLOSED the office for the day when Megan and Josh got there. But the scent of lavender oil lingered in the air as Megan led Josh through the front door and turned on the waiting room light.

"Do you want to read the literature or just get right to it?"

His smile this time had a twist of wickedness to it. "Oh, by all means, let's get to it."

Megan took Josh past the first treatment room where frolicking bunny rabbits were stenciled on the walls. There were toys in a box in one corner and a pint-sized play table and chairs in another, along with the massage and acupuncture table in the center. It was where she and Nissa treated children and it would never do for the big man who followed her.

Instead Megan opened the door on the second room and went in ahead of him, turning on that light, too.

"I'll need to test you to make sure I know exactly what you're allergic to. For that you'll have to lie on your back on the table. Shoes and socks off, please."

"I can just leave my feet hanging over the end. Then my boots won't get anything dirty."

"Your shoes and socks need to be off to do the acupuncture."

A slight frown tugged at Josh's square brow. "Guess I never really thought about it but just how much undressing does this involve?"

Megan endured a flash of temptation to tell him he had to take everything off. But she'd have a hard time explaining it once he realized it was unnecessary, so she said, "Shoes and socks off, shirt sleeves rolled up. That's all."

"I'm not too sure I like the idea of naked feet."

"It's okay, I've seen a million of them. Ones with more than five toes apiece. Ones with fewer than five toes apiece. Even a few with webs."

That skeptical expression she'd seen on his face the day they'd met returned and for a moment he just stood at the end of the treatment table staring at her.

She was pretty sure she knew what he was thinking about this time. He was thinking that maybe he wouldn't go through with the acupuncture after all.

"This is totally unprofessional," Megan said before he had the chance to bail out. "But if it would make you feel better, I'll take off my shoes and socks, too."

That idea brought out another smile, this one slow and devilish. "Okay. You first."

Megan turned her back to him. She barely raised the front of the long skirt of her dress, just enough to reach the thigh bands on each leg and roll off her tights without Josh being able to see anything. Then she slipped her feet out of her braided rope clogs and pulled the tights off, too.

The tights went into the clogs and the clogs went against the wall before she spun around again, curling up the bare toes she had no doubt Josh would be looking for.

She was right. His eyes went directly to the floor. And once more he grinned.

"Ten toes. No webs. Nice," he said.

"Your turn."

The grin widened and Megan half expected him to go on refusing to take off his own shoes and socks like a mischievous boy who'd just won a game.

But that isn't what he did.

He sat on the chair that outfitted each room for just that purpose and removed his boots and stockings. And while he did, he kept his eyes squarely on hers, as if he were one-upping her because he did it without turning his back to her.

Megan patted the table then to remind him that was where she needed him. "The method I use for testing is called applied kinesiology. Or muscle testing, because that's what it is. You lie on your back and hold small glass vials of the suspected allergens in your left hand and raise your right hand straight up in the air. If you aren't allergic to the substance, you'll be able to resist me pulling down on your right arm. If you are allergic to it, you won't be able to."

Josh had gone as far as perching a hip on the corner of the treatment table, letting one bare foot dangle but keeping the other one flat on the floor.

"You're kidding, right?" he said.

"No, I'm not kidding. It's a valid procedure."

"You think that a little vial of anything is going to make me unable to keep you from pulling my arm down?"

"If you're allergic to it. Lie down and I'll prove it to you."

He was very amused by this whole thing now. In fact, he chuckled to himself, shaking his head as if at a private joke.

It didn't bother Megan in the least.

Then he finally stretched out on the table, lying his head on the pillow and smiling up at her. "Bring it on."

"Raise your right arm."

"Without any of your magic vials?"

"Without any vials."

He did.

"Resist me," Megan instructed.

"That's what I've been tryin' and tryin' to do but I'm not havin' much luck," he said, purposely misunderstanding. Then he pretended to catch on. "Oh, you mean don't let you pull my arm down."

"Mmm," she confirmed, clasping his wrist and attempting not to notice how warm his skin was or how steely the bones she grasped. Attempting to stop the little electrical volts that skittered along her own nerve endings in response.

He's no different than any other client, she told herself.

But that wasn't easy to believe when her reaction to

him was so totally unlike any reaction she'd ever had to any other client. Or to any other man, for that matter. Including Noel.

Megan forced herself to continue in spite of it, though.

"Here we go," she said, putting all her strength into pulling his arm down.

She couldn't.

"Okay, now with the vial," she told him, taking one from the collection lined up on the top of the corner cabinet.

She handed the vial to him and said, "Ready?"

"Give it all you've got."

She didn't have to. Taking his thick wrist in her grasp the second time, she pulled his arm down as easily as the handle on a slot machine.

"Oh, come on. There's a trick to this," Josh said, his surprise ringing loud and clear.

Megan took the vial from him, had him raise his arm and resist her again, then handed the vial back to him and proceeded to once more pull his arm down.

"No trick."

"What's in the vial? Kryptonite?"

She laughed. "Are you comparing yourself to a super-hero?"

"The cape is in the car. But don't tell anybody. So what's in the vial?" he repeated.

"Plain old run-of-the-mill gasoline. It's an extremely toxic substance, which is what anything you're aller-gic to is to your body—a toxin. So the response is the same."

"And doing this kinesiology thing will tell you what I am and what I'm not allergic to?"

"Yes. What are you absolutely sure you're *not* allergic to?" she asked.

He thought about it. "Oranges."

She handed him a different vial, did the test and he was able to keep her from budging his arm from midair.

Then she gave him another vial. "Horsehair."

And again he was weakened enough for her to bring his arm all the way down to the table.

"You're definitely allergic to that."

"I don't believe it," Josh muttered.

"You told me yourself that horses made you sneeze."

"I mean I don't believe how this works."

"There are a lot of alternative medicines and treatments in the world. Western medicine isn't the be-all and end-all, you know."

Josh studied her for a long moment and Megan had the impression that he was still looking for the *trick* in what she'd done.

But then he said, "Okay. I guess we'll give it a try. But I'm still not convinced that sticking needles in me is going to make any difference."

"We have to finish the testing first," she informed him, ignoring his continuing skepticism.

It took nearly half an hour to determine that he was allergic to horsehair, hay and animal dander. But Megan explained that she could only treat him for one of the offenders per time.

Josh decided to start with hay.

"I use eight needles," Megan explained then. "One in the top of each foot, one in each shin, one in each hand in the fatty part between the thumb and the index finger, and one in each forearm. You'll have to hold several vials—the one we're clearing you for and others that strike the balance we need. You get to rest that way for twenty minutes or so—I'll leave you alone with music and the lights turned down—and then I'll come back and remove the needles, and for twenty-five hours after that you have to stay completely away from any contact with the substance to allow your system to clear and correct itself."

"Twenty-five hours?" he said as if she'd told him something outlandish. "Not twenty-six? Not nineteen? Not twenty-four hours, thirty-three minutes and eight seconds?"

"Twenty-five hours. That's just how long it takes your body to reset."

"And during that time do I have to dance around the oldest tree in town or howl at the moon when it's in its final phase?" he teased.

"You just have to stay away from hay for twenty-five hours," she said patiently. "Now why don't you roll up your sleeves while I put the needles in your feet and legs?"

"Ah, the needles again. How big are they?"

Megan showed him one after freeing it from its sterile wrapping. "It's hardly bigger than the diameter of a human hair."

He studied it suspiciously, said, "A needle is still a

needle," but finally gave her the go-ahead and Megan moved to the foot of the table.

"I'll need to push up your pant legs a little," she warned when she got there.

"Do what you have to do."

She did, edging his jeans just above mid-shin. Then she removed more needles from their wrappings and went to work.

As she did she was extremely aware of every detail of Josh's feet and lower legs. Far more aware of every detail than she'd ever been of any client before him.

His legs were thickly muscled and hairy. His ankles just a little bony. He had big feet—no shock in that since he was such a big man—but they were well cared for, free of calluses, the nails clean and cut.

He was slightly flat-footed but not that or the bony ankles mattered. It didn't even matter that what she had exposed before her was hardly the most attractive portion of anyone's anatomy. Just the sight of his naked feet, calves and ankles, the intimacy of touching him, got to Megan. She felt flushed and warm inside, and she discovered a strong craving to see more of him. To touch more of him…

But if taking off her shoes and socks had been unprofessional, it was nothing compared to those thoughts and feelings, and she told herself that in no uncertain terms.

It just didn't help much.

"That's it for down here," she announced in a quiet voice she hoped Josh would believe was part of the therapy and not an indication of what was happening to her in response to treating him.

"All the needles are in?" he asked in amazement. "I felt a tiny prick with one, I didn't think you'd done any others."

"I'll save my I-told-you-so for later," Megan said, moving to the left side of the table.

He'd rolled up his sleeves and the sight of his hands, wrists and forearms only intensified those unprofessional feelings she was having about him. Strong, powerful, capable arms and hands. And the yearning to be touched by them, held by them, hit her like a ton of bricks.

But again she tried to keep it contained and made quick work of inserting the needles on the left side. Then she moved to the right to do the same there, and once she had, she handed Josh the various vials—three in one hand, three in the other.

"I just lie here stuck with needles and holding these things now?" Josh asked as any other client might have, not sounding as if he were infected with the same sense of intimacy and fledgling desire that Megan was suffering.

"That's about it. Don't let go of the vials. Each one has to be touching skin the whole time. But other than that, you can close your eyes and relax."

"And you won't stay even if I want you to?"

Did he want her to or was he teasing her? She couldn't be sure but she knew it was better to believe he was only teasing.

"You'll rest more if you're alone and that helps your body get in tune with what it needs to do."

And maybe if she got out of that small room she could regroup.

She pushed a button on the CD player to play a recording of soft ocean sounds and dimmed the lights.

"Just rest. I'll be back in twenty minutes," she assured him, going out the door and closing it carefully behind her.

For a moment she stayed in the hallway with her hand still on the knob, deflating against the panel itself.

Why was she so vulnerable to this man? she asked herself. Why couldn't she even do her job without succumbing to some kind of primal attraction to him?

But she didn't have any answers. She just knew that she had to get control over it. Over her wandering thoughts. Over the things he made her feel. And she decided to use that twenty minutes to work on it.

So she pushed herself away from the door, set the timer she kept on a plant stand at the end of the hall, and went out the back door into the alley and the cold night air.

Clear the thoughts. Clear the feelings. Clear it all....

Too bad she couldn't perform Josh elimination acupuncture on herself, she decided.

But as much as she believed in the allergy elimination acupuncture, she didn't believe the simple application of a few needles could take away her attraction to the sheriff. For some reason he seemed to have gotten so deeply into every fiber of her being that she didn't know how to get him out of it.

But she had to keep trying, she told herself. She just had to keep trying….

Which was still what she was doing when the timer went off twenty minutes later.

Megan took a long, deep breath and held it until her lungs screamed to let it go. Then she went inside again and straight to the treatment room, ignoring the eagerness she felt to get back to him in spite of everything.

Josh's eyes were closed and didn't open until Megan turned off the CD player.

When they had, she said, "Well, did you live through it?"

"Better than that, I got a catnap."

"Good. You must have needed it," she said as she removed the needles from his feet and shins. Then she moved to the right side of the table and cupped her hands together as a sign for him to place the vials in them. He did and she set the vials on the counter before returning to the table to pull the needles from his hands and forearms, too.

"Can I get up now?" he asked.

"No reason not to. You're all done. Except for steering clear of hay for twenty-five hours. Don't forget that."

He did an effortless sit-up and got off the table, going immediately to the chair to put on his socks and boots.

Megan couldn't replace her tights as simply or as modestly as she'd been able to remove them, so she opted for not doing it at all. Instead she watched his quick, adept movements, once again feeling flushed and warm inside as she did.

"How about giving me a tour of your workplace?" Josh suggested as he stood again, still sounding nowhere near as affected by her as she was by him.

"There isn't much to see." But if she did give him the tour it meant he wouldn't be leaving immediately....

"I could show you what there is, though," she finished more brightly than she'd intended.

"I'd like to see it. This used to be my accountant's office but it looks like you did a lot of remodeling."

"Some," she confirmed as she led him out of the treatment room.

But she hadn't been kidding when she'd said there wasn't much to see. There were two more rooms exactly like the one he'd been in, the children's treatment room, a bathroom and another small alcove in the back that she and Nissa called the break room.

"This is sort of our chill-out spot," Megan explained when they ended up there. "We have the sink for water. There's that tiny refrigerator and microwave oven in the corner—mainly for lunches and snacks—and the love seat folds out in case we get stuck here for the night in a snowstorm or something."

Josh pointed to the shelves that lined one wall, full of Mason jars. "These are nothing like my accountant used to have. What's in the jars? The fixings for magic potions?" he asked as if it wouldn't surprise him if it were true.

"They're herbs, mushrooms, roots, things like that. Nissa uses them in her herbal therapies."

He took a step closer to the shelves, studying the contents of the jars. "Some of them look pretty nasty."

"That particular *nasty*-looking thing you're staring at is just ginger root. Appearances can be deceiving. But then I keep trying to tell you that."

Josh spun around on his heels to face her again. "Let's put a moratorium on that stuff for tonight, can we?"

"On what stuff?"

"On the investigation and the case of the body buried in your backyard and on you thinking you need to defend your parents and change the way I look at things. You got me in here to do the acupuncture and your needles, or lying in that room listening to water sounds, or something, made me more relaxed than I've been in a while. I'd just like to hang on to that if I could. At least for one night."

"Okay, fair enough. A moratorium," she agreed, knowing it was all the more dangerous to be with him when she didn't have the buffer of that particular conflict. But still she was only too glad to put it on the back burner herself. If even for just the moment.

"Would you like some tea?" she offered then.

He glanced over his shoulder at the jars again. "No, thanks," he said as if he were afraid she might be going to make him something from one of them.

"I have tea bags I bought from the general store," she said to reassure him.

He had the good grace to grin. "The answer's still no, thanks."

He sat on the love seat, though, and made himself at home with both arms stretched along the top of the seat back and his legs straight out and crossed at the ankles to form his body into a human—and very sexy—T.

"So what else goes on in this back room?" he asked. "Tarot card and tea leaf readings? Astrological predictions? Spells and incantations?"

"What would make you think we'd do any of that? Back here or anywhere else?"

"It's all tied in together, isn't it? The acupuncture and that Feng shui stuff you use to decorate your house. Metaphysical mumbo-jumbo."

Megan might have been insulted if that comment had come from someone with a less charming, less teasing edge to their voice. As it was, she merely propped one hip on the edge of the hip-high miniature refrigerator across from him and said, "Neither acupuncture nor Feng shui are metaphysical mumbo-jumbo. They're ancient practices. Why would they be tied to those other things?"

"They're all weird and out there—you have to admit."

"That depends completely on your point of view. Acupuncture and Feng shui are hardly *out there* in other cultures."

"And tarot cards and astrology and all that stuff? I—unfortunately—know at least one person who would argue that they're perfectly reasonable practices, too."

There was a new note to his voice. A tightness. And Megan couldn't help feeling that somehow they'd gotten to the root of something. She just didn't know what it was.

"Okay, so there are people who believe in predictions

and what-have-you, but that doesn't make it all related just because it isn't what you believe in. It isn't what *I* believe in."

"No?" he said, studying her as if he wanted to believe that but wasn't quite sure he could.

"Who do you know who's into all that other stuff? And why is it unfortunate?"

He didn't answer her right away and she could see that touching that root she thought they'd gotten to was painful for him.

But just when she thought he might not open up to her at all, he said, "My former fiancée believed in a lot of it. More than I realized until it was too late."

"I didn't know you were engaged. Or anything else about your romantic past, for that matter." But she was curious, that was for sure.

"Engaged but not married because I was left waiting at the altar."

"Oh, no."

"Oh, yes. In front of a church full of people and flowers, decked out in tuxedos, music playing, minister at the ready, the whole bit."

"What happened? And who was she? Anyone from around here?"

"Her name was Farrah Myles. She moved to town about six years ago to work in the beauty shop and I fell for her." He said that as if it had been a supreme act of stupidity. "I guess I had a clue about her right from the start—I asked her out and before she would give me an answer she wanted to know what my astrological sign was."

"And apparently it was compatible to hers."

"Right."

"And you—of all people—weren't bothered by dating-by-the-stars?" Megan joked cautiously.

"Nah. I didn't think it was any big deal. I just thought Farrah was flamboyant, fanciful, interesting—that her uniqueness went with her name. Not being run-of-the-mill was part of her appeal."

"Really?" Megan said, unable to hide her disbelief because what he was saying seemed so out of character for the man she knew him to be now.

"Really," he confirmed. "To me, until I had reason to regret it, she was endearingly quirky. Most people check their horoscopes in the newspaper or magazines when they come across them. I thought, so what if Farrah did it more religiously than that? And so what if, every now and then, she wanted her astrological chart done or read a book about bio-rhythms? It certainly never occurred to me that what I considered her hobby would rear up and bite me."

"But it did."

Josh's expression showed embarrassment. "It's bad enough to get left at the altar but when folks hear *why*..." He shook his head. "Geez. It was just so hard to fathom."

He'd finished that under his breath and Megan could see that he still bore the scars of a humiliation that had to have been difficult for him to accept.

"Why did she leave you at the altar?" she asked, hoping he wouldn't think she was prying. At least not too much.

Again Josh didn't answer instantly. And when he did it was with a mirthless snort of a chuckle preceding it. "She called her psychic the day of the wedding and he told her not to go through with it. That she was destined for someone else."

"You're kidding?"

"Her *psychic* told her she was meant to marry someone of East Indian descent who was to be found in Los Angeles. And that if she went through with marrying me it would be a disaster bad enough to keep her from ever finding true love and happiness."

"And she believed that so completely that she actually called off your wedding at the last minute?" Megan asked, unable to keep her own incredulity out of her tone.

"*Called* is the right word. Farrah called the church and said she was sorry but the wedding wasn't going to happen. Just like that, as if it were nothing."

"No wonder you're so suspicious of anything out of the norm."

Josh inclined his head and laughed a little, this time genuinely, even if it was tinged with wryness. "There's a lot to be said for conservatism. I swore to myself that if I lived through the jokes and ridicule that came out of being left at the altar because someone's psychic pal told them not to marry me, I'd stick to the tried and true."

"But if no one ever ventured outside of the tried and true a lot of important, helpful things might be overlooked rather than used where they could be the most beneficial."

There was still skepticism on his face and it was to

that that she said, "Acupuncture really is not the same as astrological charts and tarot card readings and biorhythms and psychic predictions, you know."

Megan wasn't sure why it meant so much to her to have him make the distinction. She knew it shouldn't have mattered to her one way or another.

But it did.

Josh smiled then and seemed to be sloughing off the darker mood that had settled over him while he'd talked about his past. "We'll see if there's more to the acupuncture than that other stuff, won't we?" he said, back to playfully goading her.

Then he glanced at his watch and stood. "I'd better get going. If I can't be anywhere near hay, I can't sleep at the ranch tonight. That means I'll have to drop in on my brother Jace and see if he and his new wife will put me up in town. I don't want to get there and spring it on them too late."

Or maybe thinking about that flighty woman who had left him at the altar had reminded him of all the reasons he didn't want to be around a woman he seemed to put in the same category.

But there was nothing Megan could do about that and, as disappointed as it left her, she didn't argue.

She pushed off the edge of the table. "I'll walk you out so I can lock the door after you."

"You're not headed for home, too?"

"Shortly. I have a couple of things I want to do first." Namely put her shoes and tights back on.

"We need to get an early start in the morning," Josh

said on the way to the waiting room. "Hopefully we won't run into any hay in the coin shops of Cheyenne."

Megan had nearly forgotten that that was what they were scheduled to do the next day. But the reminder that she was already scheduled to see him again helped ease the disappointment of having him leave now. Slightly, anyway.

"Just tell me when and I'll be ready," she said as if their plans had never slipped her mind.

"How about seven? Then even with the drive time we should have the whole day."

"Fine."

Josh opened the office door and stepped outside. But he didn't go farther than the doorway before turning and leaning a shoulder against the jamb.

"Are there side effects I should be looking for from your torture of me?" he asked with a teasing smile that was charming enough to make his words inoffensive.

"Nope. That's part of the advantage of acupuncture."

"I have to admit you must be good at it because I really didn't feel much of anything."

"And no burns on your palms from the kryptonite in the vials?" she joked in return.

He held his hands out, palms upward, and presented them to her for examination. "I don't know, what do you think?"

The urge to touch him again was suddenly overwhelming and Megan had to give in to it. She ran her index finger along one of his palms as if testing for injuries.

Maybe it tickled him because in response his hand closed almost reflexively around her finger. But once it had he held on tight.

"I don't feel any kryptonite burns," she said, her voice soft and far more sensual than she'd intended.

Josh let go of her finger only enough to entwine all of his through all of hers. Then he pulled her towards him a little and Megan looked from their clasped hands to his face.

His expression was serious again, although not the way it had been when he'd talked about his former fiancée. Now he merely seemed intent as his eyes delved into hers.

He didn't say anything. But then neither did she. He just pulled her the rest of the way to him and leaned in to kiss her much the way he had the night before.

But if the kiss the night before had been good—so good she'd been left momentarily stunned by it—it was still nothing compared to this one.

His lips were parted over hers, urging hers to part, too, as his arms came around her and held her so close he brought her up onto her toes.

She'd wanted his arms around her. She'd yearned for it. And yet even that yearning and the fantasies of what it might be like didn't compare to the reality.

His arms were strong and powerful, unyielding but gentle, surrounding her in the warm cocoon of his muscular body and making her feel removed from everything but the pleasure of being enveloped by him. Kissed by him.

And while a tiny voice somewhere in the back of her

mind said she should push him away, she slid her arms around him, too, filling her hands with the steely wall of his back.

His tongue began to tease her then. Just the tip. Running along the oh-so-sensitive bare inside of her lips and tickling her the way she'd wondered if her finger had tickled his palm. It almost made her laugh but instead she let her tongue meet his for some teasing of its own.

One of his hands floated up to the back of her head, cradling it as he pressed forward, as he parted his lips even farther and urged hers to part farther, too.

She obliged, thinking only about him now, about that kiss and how much she liked it. About how incredible it felt to be in his strong arms, to have her breasts against his chest, her nipples kerneling into the solid wall of his pectorals.

Now *this* is unprofessional, she thought as it crossed her mind that they were in her office doorway, right on Center Street and in plain view of anyone and everyone within blocks.

But she didn't really care. She was too lost in that kiss, in those arms and that towering masculine body she craved to know even more intimately as desire ignited from the tiny sparks he'd lit the moment he'd closed his fist around her finger. Tiny sparks that had grown hotter with each increment of mouths opening wider and wider, with each thrust of his tongue, with each answering parry of hers, with each massage of his hand at her back when it was really her front that cried out for his touch…

Come back inside, she willed him because she didn't want to say it. Saying it would mean she would have to end that kiss. She would have to lose the pure luxury of his mouth over hers, maybe even of his arms from around her. *Just come back inside....*

But apparently they weren't on the same wavelength when it came to that because rather than returning to the seclusion of the office's break room the way Megan was imagining, Josh began to rewind.

His tongue became less insistent, more playful, then retreated altogether. His mouth left hers, returning with only barely parted lips a time or two, before ending the kissing completely.

But he didn't let her go. He just dropped his chin to the top of her head and stayed that way for a time, breathing hot, sweet air into her hair.

"I hope this isn't how you say goodbye to all your acupuncture patients," he joked after another moment, his voice husky enough to let her know he wasn't taking that kiss any more lightly than she was despite the fact that he'd called a halt to it when that was the last thing she'd wanted.

"I hope this isn't how you say goodbye to all the children of your prime suspects," she countered.

"Only the pretty ones."

She laughed at that, still wanting him to stay, to come back inside with her, to kiss her and hold her and touch her....

She heard him inhale, long and deep, feeling his lungs expand, bringing his chest and her breasts into even closer contact for another moment before he exhaled and left her aching for more.

"I have to get out of here," he said as if it was the last thing he wanted to do.

But then he took his arms away and clasped her shoulders in each big hand, bending to kiss the center of her forehead at her hairline before holding her in place while he took a step back, onto the boardwalk and let her go completely.

"See you in the morning," he said, the hushed raspiness of his voice the only indication of what they'd just shared.

"See you in the morning," she whispered because it was as much as she could summon.

He held up one index finger and touched her top lip with it, lingering for only a split second, and then yanking his hand to his chest as if it were the only way he was going to keep from taking hold of her and pulling her into his arms again.

And even as every nerve in her body shrieked for him to do just that, Megan watched him get into his car to go.

He started the engine and put it into gear, all with his eyes still on her. But he didn't move from his parking spot. Instead he went on staring at her as if he might not leave after all.

Then he held up one hand in a wave and finally backed onto Center Street, and Megan watched him drive off.

It was only after he had that she realized she was still

standing in her doorway, in her bare feet, with her toes curled to the sky.

She made herself turn and go back into the office. But as she did she couldn't help wondering if she really had learned her lesson with men.

It seemed as if every moment she spent with Josh—in spite of how hard she tried to fight it—only made her more vulnerable. Vulnerable to the attraction she had for him. Vulnerable to feelings that kept cropping up and getting stronger despite her attempt to restrain them. Vulnerable to desires that seemed to have a life of their own. Vulnerable to the man himself.

And that scared her.

Because clearly Josh Brimley was a man who might never be comfortable with anything but the tried and true.

A man who might never be comfortable with someone who didn't swim in the mainstream.

With someone like her...

Chapter 8

UNTIL ABOUT THREE O'CLOCK the next afternoon, Megan was worried that the trip to Cheyenne to canvas coin dealers was nothing more than a wild goose chase. If the coins had existed at all and been sold, Cheyenne was hardly the only place that transaction could have occurred even if it was the biggest city nearest to Elk Creek. And since she and Josh had a list of shops that stretched from one end of the city to the other in every direction and not any of the first eleven they visited had ever seen anything but pictures of gold doubloons, she didn't have a lot of confidence in their quest.

But just as both she and Josh were acknowledging that the trip might have been a waste of time, that if the coins had existed and anyone had sold them, they must have done it somewhere farther away from Elk Creek than Cheyenne, they hit pay dirt with store number twelve.

"Didn't buy 'em myself," the shop owner said. He was an extremely tall, string-bean-skinny man with a head full of white hair. "Couldn't put out that kind of money when I was just startin' and already had loans up to my eyeballs to get myself goin'. But I did broker the sale."

"Eighteen years ago?" Josh said as if testing to make sure this fit the bill.

The shop owner pointed over his shoulder to the wall behind him where frames held licenses to operate. "That's how long I been in business. Eighteen years. Those doubloons were one of my first deals. Helped launch me."

"Do you have records of the sale?" Josh asked.

"From eighteen years ago? Nooo. I only keep 'em as long as the tax man says I have to. Papers from that far back are history."

"Do you remember the person or people who brought the coins in? A name? Anything?"

"Don't remember your name and you just told it to me. It's faces I'm good with. Never forget a face."

Megan had a photograph of her parents in her wallet and she took it out to show the dealer. "Do either of these people look familiar?"

The man peered at the picture when Megan handed it to him, studying it closely. "Nah. Besides, the guy with the doubloons was older'n this all those years ago." The dealer raised one finger then as light apparently dawned. "And he had a limp. I remember that now. Said it was a war injury. Don't know which war, though."

"Would the person you sold the coins to have any more information on the seller?" Josh asked.

"They never met. I was the go-between, that's how I earned my part. I had the only contact with the owner of the doubloons and there wasn't much to even that.

He was in a hurry to sell, said he needed money fast, so I took care of it fast."

"And there was nothing about it that struck you as suspicious?"

"No, sir. I always do it by the book so I know I made 'im show identification and sign off sayin' he was the rightful owner. If there'd of been anything suspicious about it I would have called in the authorities, but there must not of been."

"And all that paperwork is gone?" Josh said as if hoping he hadn't heard it right the first time.

"Like I said."

The coin dealer assured them that there was nothing more he could tell them. But Josh left him a business card just in case anything else came to mind and asked for one from the dealer, complete with his name, and his home address and phone number to go with the business information.

Then Josh and Megan left.

"So the dealer not only didn't recognize my parents, he's a witness to the fact that a man much older than my father sold the coins," Megan said victoriously as they got into Josh's squad car in the parking lot beside the shop. "Now will you take my parents off the suspect list?"

"Not completely," Josh answered as he started the engine, pulled out of his parking spot and then out of the lot.

"Why not completely?"

"Because it could have been Chaney himself who sold the coins and then was killed for the money," Josh said reasonably as he maneuvered through the traffic of downtown Cheyenne.

"I don't think so. If Chaney hadn't sold the coins before that, why would he have sold them then? I think he liked having the coins themselves. They made for a better story. And certainly they were easier to cart around with him and hide than a whole lot of cash would have been. Besides, why would he need money all of a sudden? He was a drifter and there was no indication that he was tired of that or wanted any other kind of life. My dad said that Chaney told him he was ready to move on and that Chaney was walking down the road as we drove off."

"But anything your father says is suspect," Josh pointed out. "Maybe Chaney had decided to settle down and was going to buy your place from your folks before you all left. And maybe, rather than selling it to him, they opted for getting rid of Chaney, taking the money and still hanging onto the property."

"Because they're master-mind criminals," Megan added facetiously. "You just won't give up on them, will you?"

Josh looked at her out of the corner of his striking blue eyes and smiled a smile that let her know he was enjoying the debate too much to concede.

But then he conceded anyway. If only slightly. "I'll admit this information expands the suspicion a little. Chaney's bones didn't indicate any reason he would have had a limp or anything that looked like an old war injury."

"So you don't think whoever sold the coins was my father *or* Chaney."

"Let's just say this sheds a new light on things. I want to check past medical records in town, see if there's anything about Chaney maybe spraining his ankle when he was in Elk Creek. That could account for a limp and he might have made up the war injury story just to seem interesting or maybe play on sympathies to get himself a better deal. At the very least we now have a couple things to look into that we didn't have before."

"What else besides the medical records?"

"I can get access to the Defense Department's database through the Internet and find out if Chaney had a military record."

"Okay. So if Chaney didn't have a medical record or a military record then it looks like he didn't sell the coins himself. We know my father didn't sell the coins, and if Chaney didn't have money for him to steal, then you have more reason to stop suspecting my folks of anything at all," Megan concluded, again victoriously. "And if we head back to Elk Creek right now we can check both those things today."

"I was thinking of buying you dinner in Cheyenne tonight. For a change."

"Let's do this and I'll fix you dinner," she said as a trade-off.

"Tofu salad and bean sprouts?"

"Whatever you want."

"Whatever?" he repeated, adding innuendo to the single word.

"Just head for home and we'll negotiate that later," she ordered.

But the excitement in her tone wasn't entirely due to the fact that she felt on the verge of clearing her parents' good name.

Dinner ended up being takeout from the only restaurant in Elk Creek besides the Dairy King—Margie Wilson's Café. Megan and Josh ate at Josh's desk in the sheriff's office after having failed to come up with any local medical records on Pete Chaney.

As they did, Josh searched the Defense Department's databases while Megan did another job he hadn't yet had the time to get to—she placed calls to Nebraska trying to find any relatives Chaney might have had there.

It was late when they both finally finished and as Megan hung up the phone Josh stretched his long arms into the air, arched his back until it cracked and then propped his feet on the corner of the desk, crossing them at the ankles.

"No more," he said as if crying uncle.

Megan agreed and rolled her head in a circle trying to ease the crick in her neck.

"What did you come up with?" she asked when the head-circles failed to help and she ended up looking at Josh across the desk.

"You show me yours and I'll show you mine," he said, his expression a more mature—and infinitely more appealing—version of an ornery schoolboy.

He'd taken a break a few hours earlier and returned from his office bathroom free of the five o'clock shadow that had roughened his jaw so he still looked neat and clean and smelled of that aftershave that Megan liked more than she wanted to think about. His antique-oak-colored hair was too short to get mussed but it was somewhat more spiky on top from unconsciously dragging his hands through it the way she'd surreptitiously caught him doing a few times as he'd worked on the computer.

His uniform shirt seemed as fresh as it had been early that morning when he'd picked her up at home, but he'd rolled the sleeves to his elbows, exposing wrists and forearms that Megan found sexier than she would ever have believed possible. And, as always, just one glance at those blue eyes of his, at the sharp, masculine perfection of his features, and she found it more difficult than it should have been to think clearly.

But she worked at it, recalling that in his all-too-insinuating way he'd asked what she'd found out about Pete Chaney's connection with Nebraska.

"I called every Chaney listed in the current phone book," she finally said. "But not one of them had ever heard of a Pete or a Peter Chaney.

"And none of them had any relatives that were unaccounted for. I also did what you told me and asked a Nebraska librarian to use the reverse directory to get the telephone number for the address on his expired driver's license. When I called the number the librarian gave me, the woman I spoke to said she'd lived in the house for the last fifteen years. She bought it from two elderly spinster sisters named Blanchard, and I couldn't contact them because they've both passed away."

"So nothing."

"So nothing. What about you?"

"I knew Chaney didn't have a criminal record in Wyoming but I'd put out a nation-wide inquiry and my answer was here when I turned on the computer. He came up clean all the way around. He did enlist in the army, but he went AWOL during boot camp and that's the last the army ever saw of him. But the information on his enlistment papers shows the same address as his driver's license and names no next of kin at all—which I guess pretty much jibes with your finding no Chaneys who knew or were related to him."

"And that's it? Between the two of us all we found out was that Pete Chaney effectively disappeared long before he actually disappeared?"

"Looks like it. Well, that and that he didn't have anyone who cared if he disappeared and also didn't have a war injury—or any other injury to speak of—that might have made him limp. Plus I put in a call to Buzz Martindale while you were washing your hands and he didn't recall Chaney having a limp either."

"So it was someone else who sold the coin and my folks are off the hook," Megan concluded.

"Let's just say they're a step closer to being off the hook. But there are still the possibilities we talked about before—your parents could have taken the coins and had a friend sell them, or Chaney could have had a friend sell them and your folks could have done him in for the money the friend brought back."

Megan did a frustrated squeal. "You really just never give up, do you?"

Josh grinned at her and reminded in a confidential tone that lifted his chiseled chin, "The body was buried in their backyard. I can't just give up on them."

Megan closed her eyes and shook her head. "Oh fine," she muttered, too weary by then to argue the point anymore.

"Ready for another moratorium?" Josh asked, correctly reading her concession.

"For tonight I am."

"Good. Me, too. Want to get some fresh air?"

They hadn't spent more than five minutes apart all day and evening yet anything that prolonged her time with him was welcome to Megan. Although she didn't want him to know that so she tried to keep her enthusiasm to a minimum.

"I'm not dressed for too much of the night air but a little would be nice," she answered, referring to the brown cargo pants and matching V-neck sweater she wore, and the fact that despite it having been a particularly warm April day, the temperature outside was still not likely to be balmy.

"We'll run the car heater on the way and I'll keep you warm when we get to where I want to take you," he promised.

"When we get to where you want to take me? That sounds interesting."

"Might be. We'll just have to see. But one way or another I'll make sure you don't freeze to death."

There was that promise again and she knew it was fraught with danger.

But it was also too tempting to pass up regardless of

how many red flags waved in Megan's mind to warn her that passing it up was exactly what she *should* do.

"Okay," she heard herself say a little more eagerly than she intended.

"Great."

Josh dropped his feet to the floor, shut down the computer and stood with what seemed like renewed energy. "Let's go then."

On the way to the squad car parked alongside the courthouse building they encountered a couple Josh stopped to introduce her to—Kate McDermot and her new husband Brady Brown.

When the amenities were complete, Josh extended his congratulations on the recent announcement of their pregnancy. That prompted Megan to ask to hold the other woman's hand.

"I'm nearly a hundred percent right in telling the sex if I touch the mother's hand," Megan explained matter-of-factly to the three people in various stages of curiosity and amusement.

"Okay," Kate McDermot agreed.

Megan clasped Kate's hand like any friend happy to see her and then let go again to pronounce, "It's a girl."

"My doctor is betting on it being a boy from the speed of the heartbeat," Kate informed her.

"He's wrong," Megan said with confidence, making them all laugh.

"I'm your witness," Josh told the other couple. "If you paint the room pink and then have a boy I'll make her come in and repaint it blue."

"It's a deal," Brady said.

The four of them chatted a moment more and then went their separate ways. As they did, Josh said, "I thought you didn't play psychic?"

"I don't. I'm just really good at baby predictions for some reason."

"Mmm-hmm," he said with another laugh as he held open her door for her when they reached the patrol car. "Guess we'll see," he added before he closed the door and rounded the rear of the car to get behind the wheel.

He started the engine and backed out of the parking spot, then he said, "So, speaking of Farrah—"

It was Megan's turn to laugh. "I didn't know we were."

"Psychics, predictions, Farrah—it's all tied up to-gether in my mind. So, speaking of Farrah, I aired my dirty laundry for you, now how about telling me why there isn't a tree-hugger husband and a passel of nature-loving kids in your life?"

"Now *that* was a segue," Megan said with another laugh.

Josh smiled sheepishly at her. "Okay, maybe it wasn't too smooth. But I've been wondering and smooth or not, I'd still like to know."

"I'd like to have kids but not a *passel*. Two kids—that's all I'll have so I don't contribute to the earth's overpopulation," she said, purposely omitting an answer to what she knew he was more interested in—her ro-mantic past.

"Not more than two kids. Of course," Josh said. "But what about the tree-hugger husband?"

Megan's smile at his persistence was smug. But she decided not to make him work any harder for that answer. "I was engaged until not very long ago. Like you, except it ended before we got to the altar."

"Who, what, when, where, why?"

"Nosy," she joked.

"Part of the job, ma'am," he responded as if that were the only reason for his inquiry.

"His name is Noel Mikeljon and he's a corporate attorney."

"A corporate attorney? Didn't that make him the enemy?"

"It made him unlike most of my close acquaintances, yes," Megan conceded. "But the corporation he works for is a software company, not a polluter, so he was okay."

"How'd you meet him?"

"There was a labor dispute and Nissa and I and our folks had joined a group that came out in support of the union. Noel and I literally bumped into each other on the street."

"You were picketing and he was trying to get to work," Josh guessed.

Megan had to laugh at his accuracy. "As a matter of fact. But the labor dispute was settled fairly—thanks in large part to Noel—so—"

"You were welcome to bring him back to the remodeled school bus to meet Mom and Dad."

"Yes," Megan said with another laugh. "Although

the remodeled school bus died about ten years ago and they bought a motor home."

"But still, one thing led to another…" Josh prompted her to go on.

"One thing led to another and we got engaged."

"But…"

"But I learned that even if opposites attract, they just don't mesh in the long run."

"Meaning?"

"Noel was the poster boy for straight arrows but I thought it was sort of cute. I thought I'd loosen him up and we'd be a good mix."

"But there was no bending the arrow?"

"You'd think that after a whole lifetime of my family being considered freaks that I would have known better. That I would have known that someone with a closed mind is not likely to open it. But at first he hid how really embarrassed he was by my family—and by me, too, I guess."

"He was *embarrassed* by you?"

"Don't sound so shocked. You were *embarrassed* by your former fiancée, as I recall."

"I was embarrassed to be left waiting for her at the altar. And I was embarrassed after that to have to tell people that she did it because her psychic had told her to. Show me anyone who wouldn't have been embarrassed by that. But I was never ashamed of her, and it sounds to me like that's really what you're talking about."

It was funny but until Josh put it that way, Megan hadn't thought of it in terms of shame. But now that she did, she realized he was right.

"I suppose embarrassment was just an easier word to swallow than shame, but really, shame is more on the money," she admitted quietly. "Noel was basically ashamed of me, of my family, of what I think he eventually came to consider lowering himself to be with me."

"So what was this Noel guy doing anywhere near you under those circumstances?"

"Initially I think dating me made him feel like James Dean. It seemed rebellious. As if I was proof that he had a wild streak or something."

"Because he was going out with *you?*" Josh laughed as they headed out past the farms and ranches to the west of Elk Creek into the open countryside. "So eating organic and recycling was this guy's idea of living on the edge?"

"Something like that. At least I was well-outside his circle."

"And your plan to loosen him up?"

"Failed miserably. Instead what started to happen was a lot of him trying hard to change me. He was subtle about it and it was always couched in what seemed to be a desire just to help me see a better way, but he didn't like my jewelry or my clothes or my hair—"

Josh took his eyes off the road to look her up and down. "What was wrong with any of that?"

"According to Noel, tasteful pearls, conservative diamonds, or the occasional lapel pin, were all any woman should wear for jewelry. Beads—" Megan held up her left wrist where she wore a string of tan-and-black speckled beads "—were déclassé. My *wispy* dresses—as

he called them—looked like they belonged in a schoolyard. And my hair should be worn any way that was
smooth—buns, ponytails, French knots, even loose was
okay, but he hated it when I twisted it and let the ends
spike."

"Would this have been acceptable?" Josh asked, nodding at her hair.

She'd sectioned the sides and top and pulled each
section back to her crown in small tortoiseshell clips.

"No, Noel would have preferred a simple
headband."

Josh leaned slightly toward her, eyes back on the road,
and whispered, "I think you look great."

"Thanks," she said, and even though the compliment
had been offhand it still pleased her.

"So what was the straw that broke the camel's
back?" he asked then. "You couldn't agree on a wedding dress?"

"It wasn't only the way I looked that was the problem.
He also didn't want me telling people I was an acupuncturist. He wanted me to say I was in the health-care
profession. And there were a lot of other things. He
certainly didn't want me to talk about how I'd grown up.
I was supposed to say I was from Wyoming and leave it
at that. And I was never to take issue over anything with
anyone I met in connection with him even if the person
openly dumped raw sewage into the nearest water source
and bragged about it."

"Maybe he wanted a robot, not a woman."

"Maybe. But believe it or not, he was so subtle, so
diplomatic, so much on my side when he said these

things that I didn't really put it all together until we were talking about actually getting married. That was when I finally figured out that he didn't think we should elope because it would be romantic and spontaneous, he thought we should elope so his family and friends wouldn't have to meet my folks."

"Nice."

"It opened my eyes to what was going on. I'd let myself be convinced that all his helpful hints about my clothes, my hair, my jewelry, what I did and didn't say, were to protect me from the small-mindedness of his friends and family. But the reality of it was that it was Noel who was small-minded, Noel who was embarrassed—no, ashamed of me. That Noel was just trying to protect himself, trying to fit me into that same mold he was in, trying to change who I am."

"That must have hurt," Josh said compassionately.

"It definitely hurt. It hurt most because I was so fooled by him. Because along the way I honestly didn't think he was criticizing me himself. And then, when I had my eyes opened to it, it was such a slap in the face to realize what he thought of me, that it was all so negative. So disparaging. That he was *ashamed* of me."

Megan's voice dwindled off just as Josh pulled from the main road onto a dirt one devoid of all street lights.

He reached over and took her hand from where it rested in her lap and squeezed it comfortingly. "Sounds to me like you got out in the nick of time."

"Is that how you felt about being left at the altar? That you got out in the nick of time?"

"Not at that very second I didn't, no. Or right after. But once I got some perspective, yeah, I started to see that I was better off without someone who would let something like a random psychic prediction rule her. Do you regret not ending up with this Noel guy?"

"No," Megan said without having to think about it. "I'm sorry that he turned out to be the kind of person he was, and that the whole thing was so painful, but I look at not ending up with him as a good thing. Imagine how awful it would have been to marry him, maybe even have a child—"

"Or two."

"Or two—with him, and then to find out he was ashamed of me and my family."

"That would *not* have been a good thing."

"I just felt so stupid," she confided in an extremely quiet voice, something she hadn't shared with anyone before.

Josh was still holding her hand and he squeezed it again. "I know all about that," he commiserated.

Then he let go of her hand so he could turn off the car lights as he slowed their speed to a snail's crawl.

"Maybe we should call a moratorium on talking about this subject, too," Josh suggested. "After all, we came out here to *un*wind, not to *re*wind."

"Fine by me," Megan agreed, curious now about where he was taking her. "What are we doing out here?"

"It's a surprise. Or maybe it's nothing. Depends on our timing," he said in a hushed voice, as if to speak louder would somehow disturb something.

They were in the middle of nowhere when he stopped the patrol car and turned off the engine. The only illumination was from the moon and the stars but since it was such a clear night and they'd long since left any artificial light behind, Megan's eyes adjusted and she could see fairly well.

At least she could see there wasn't much of anything to see.

On either side of them was flat, open ground. Slightly up ahead was a single, generations-old elm tree, and beyond that was a small pond and a slight rise into the foothills that would become the Rocky Mountains.

Josh pointed a long, thick index finger at the tree. "That's our goal. But it's important that we get to it as quietly as possible. So from here on, only whispers and soft steps."

He got out of the car, closing the door with infinite care so it made no noise whatsoever. Then he came around to help Megan out and to do the same thing with her door.

Once he had he took her hand again and held a finger to his lips before taking her across the distance to the tree.

Early in its life the trunk of the elm had split into three, forming a triple-pronged lee about two feet from its base. It was in that lee that Josh positioned himself. Then he situated Megan directly in front of him.

When he had her just where he wanted her, he brought both arms around her and pulled her gently backward until she was braced against him and enveloped in the warmth of his big body.

Again that single finger pointed, this time to the pond not ten feet in front of them, as he whispered into her ear, "There's a herd of wild mustangs that come down here to water most nights. If they don't catch our scent we'll get to see them."

Megan didn't much care whether or not the horses showed up. It felt so wonderful to be in Josh's arms, to feel the heat of his breath against her skin and in her hair, to feel the solidity of his honed pectorals behind her back, that nothing else really mattered to her at that moment. As far as she was concerned, even if the horses never appeared, the evening had taken a turn for the better and she merely leaned into Josh and let every pore soak up the sensation of him holding her.

But the mustangs did come.

Only a few minutes later, just as all the stress and tension of the day, of recalling her relationship with Noel and its demise, drained away, the thunderous sound of hooves echoed from a canyon amidst the foothills, and the shadows and stillness before Megan and Josh suddenly came to life.

Megan counted fourteen horses, each one more beautiful than the last as they slowed to a trot and came to the edges of the pond to drink.

Moonlight gleamed off their sleek backs, their powerful haunches, their proud manes. Tails were high. And pure, unfettered energy filled the night air.

Megan and Josh stayed motionless and silent, watching them.

When the horses had their fill of the fresh, clear water, some wandered off to munch early spring grass while others—the colts—played. Frolicked, actually, snorting and butting heads, rearing up on their hind legs to paw the air in a blustery show of prowess.

After a while, two of the mustangs separated themselves from the rest and came nearer to where Megan and Josh were camouflaged by the tree. It was impossible to tell for sure in the dim light, but it seemed obvious that one was a mare and the other a stallion.

Unlike the bravado and roughness of the colts, these two nudged and nuzzled noses, playfully, shyly at first, then more boldly, but never with the rigor of the younger animals.

"I think he's wooing her," Josh barely whispered into Megan's ear.

But whether it was enough for the stallion to hear, or that the slight movement had drawn his attention, the mustang's ears perked up and his head tilted in their direction. He froze like that for just a split second, then he lunged sideways away from that spot and his lady-love.

Apparently it was a signal to them all because the mare followed fast on his heels and so did the rest of the horses. Suddenly the whole herd was in motion, a symphony of long, graceful legs carrying dark streaks through the night, back the way they'd come, back into the shadows, into the hills, the sound of their hooves receding until nothing was left but the quiet and stillness again.

"Looks like I blew it," Josh said then, his voice a normal timbre now that it didn't matter anymore.

"Maybe they'll come back," Megan said even though

she knew they wouldn't. It was just that she was loathe to break the closeness she was sharing with Josh, loathe to lose the warm cocoon of his body.

"Nah, once they're spooked they'll stay away," he said.

But he must not have been any more eager to move from the relative seclusion of that spot than Megan was because he didn't budge. Instead he stayed there, holding her against him from behind.

"Are you cold?" he asked then, as if that might be the deciding factor.

The three-trunk tree seemed to provide some insulation and that, coupled with Josh's body, was enough to keep the chill of the night air away. Still though, Megan knew she should say she was freezing so they could go back to his car, back to town, and to their separate homes without anything more happening between them.

But what she knew and what she wanted were two different things....

"No, I'm not cold at all. What about you?" she asked, thinking that maybe he'd have the willpower she lacked and that she'd offer him the opportunity to use it.

But rather than exhibiting any signs of it, he said, "Nope. Feelin' fine. Just fine," and not only was his tone full of innuendo, his arms tightened around her to pull her even closer against him.

The last of her tension seemed to have fled with the mustangs and all that remained was a sense of utter contentment. Of course she recognized that that was the last thing she should be feeling with Josh Brimley, but her contentment was so complete that she couldn't make herself care any more than she could make herself push away from him.

And in response to that contentment, Megan let her head rest against his shoulder.

"This is nice," she said quietly.

"I come out here when I need to get away. To forget about things for a while."

"It works."

"I know."

And maybe what they were both forgetting was that they shouldn't be doing this.

But there was a deep richness to Josh's voice that told her that holding her like that was having as much effect on him as it was on her. Which was no small thing as the faint scent of his aftershave tantalized her, as her body seemed to melt into his, as her thoughts turned to more than merely standing there....

His thoughts must have been going in the same direction because he kissed the side of her neck then.

His mouth was like velvet as he lingered there, his breath warm and soft. It was nothing really. And yet it was enough to set off a rain of glitter that went all through her as he kissed a path upward, each soft touch of his mouth another infusion of that glitter until, by the time he brought his hand to cup her cheek and turn her head to him, Megan felt as if she were sparkling on the inside.

His mouth came over hers, his lips already parted in a kiss that wasn't teasing or playful or tentative tonight. A kiss that was serious from the start.

Which was exactly how Megan answered it, parting her own lips in welcome, moving in his arms so she was more accessible, raising a hand to the side of his face.

His tongue began an exploration of the tender inner edges of her lips. Of the very tips of her teeth. Of her tongue. Searching. Seeking a partner.

And Megan was only too willing to oblige. To meet him halfway, to do the dance they did so well together even if they were new to it.

She was only too willing for anything and everything. For being pressed into the cradle of one eminently able arm. For the feathery strokes of the hand that had eased her face around for his kiss and now worked its way along the column of her neck, easing downward so slowly it was nearly imperceptible.

Too slowly, actually. Because there was nothing Megan wanted more at that moment than to be touched by him. Than to have his hands on her. On her bare flesh. On her breasts.

Breasts that were straining for attention. Crying for it. For him.

Megan trailed her own hand from his face to the strong cords of his neck, to his collarbone, to the hard bulge of his pectorals.

She didn't mean it as a hint but only in response to her own thoughts of where she wanted his hand to be. And even if she had intended it as a hint it didn't matter because Josh kept his own pace in the soothing stroke of fingertips that glided along her neck, that dipped into the hollow of her throat, that traced her breastbone only to the V of her sweater and back again as his mouth opened wide over hers and their kisses grew more feverish, more fervent, more frenzied.

Feverish and fervent and frenzied enough so that what had begun as a yearning for him to reach her breasts became a need so deep it turned her nipples into hardened knots that ached for his attention.

This time it was by design that she let her own hand slip inside the open collar of Josh's shirt, toying with the buttons until they opened. One by one. Until she could reach inside to his bare chest.

But what had started as his cue changed almost instantly to her own pleasure as she made contact with his satin-over-steel skin, with the slight smattering of coarse hair, with his own male nibs kerneling beneath her fingers.

Not only was he spectacular but it was as if there was a sensuality simmering just beneath the surface. A sensuality that, once unleashed, made every inch of him feel charged with it. Charging her with it in return.

And Megan *was* charged with it. That glitter he'd sent through her with his first kiss seemed to burst like fireworks on the Fourth of July, awakening every sense, every nerve ending Megan possessed.

As if Josh knew just how ready she was, that was when his hand made a more purposeful descent, finding its way inside the V neck of her sweater, inside the lacy cup of her bra.

Maybe this was why women gave up wearing bras altogether, she thought. Because she wanted so much for it to disappear, for Josh to be able to touch her without any restraint.

Not that that restraint mattered much, though, when he finally cupped her breast in the warm kid-leather of his palm. When he began to knead that oh-so-alive globe and tease her yearning nipple with adept fingers that gently rolled it, pinched it, followed the ultra-sensitive aureole with just the bare tips.

It felt so good. So, so incredibly good that Megan had to tear her mouth away from his just to take in more air as all he was arousing in her robbed her of breath.

But as if he wasn't already driving her wild enough, his mouth began the same downward trip his hand had taken as he raised her breast up and out of her bra, nuzzling her sweater below it at the same time so he could enclose her in the dark cavern of that mouth she'd abandoned.

She couldn't help the moan that escaped her throat in response. Couldn't help digging her fingers slightly into his chest and arching her spine to allow him a freer course.

She was nearly out of her mind with wanting him. With wanting all of him in a way she'd never felt so intensely before. Not even with Noel.

Noel…

Oh, what an awful time for him to invade her thoughts!

But once he had there came with him the memory of how different the two of them had been. The reminder that they'd been as different as she and Josh were.

And how much she'd been hurt by those differences in the past. How much she could be hurt by the differences between her and Josh now. Especially if she let this go where her entire body, her entire being, was crying out for it to go.

But how could she deny herself the wonders he was evoking with his hands, with his mouth, with his body pressed against hers?

Not easily, that was for sure.

But as much as she wanted him, as much as she wanted more of him, that's how afraid she was of being hurt by him the way she'd been hurt by Noel.

So she drew in a deep breath and breathed it out in a shaky exhalation before saying, "I think we better stop."

Josh did just that, although not abruptly enough to make it easy for Megan to stick to her resolve. He pressed a heated kiss to the crest of her breastbone, then to the hollow of her throat again, then to the side of her neck just below her jaw, then to her chin and finally one last kiss to her lips as he pulled her so close that her bared breast pressed to his chest where it was exposed by his shirt front.

"Should I not have done that? Should I apologize?" he asked in a raspy whisper, dropping his brow to the top of her head.

"No. I wanted…" She almost said *I wanted you* but caught herself and amended it to, "There's nothing to apologize for. I just didn't want it to go too far."

Josh nodded and she wasn't sure whether the nod meant that he agreed that they shouldn't go too far or just to let her know he understood now why she'd called a halt to what had been happening between them.

"Guess the mustangs weren't the only wild things out here tonight," he joked.

Megan managed a weak smile but it required effort as her blood went on racing through her veins as if the message that it should slow down hadn't yet reached it. "Maybe it's something in the air."

Josh didn't say anything for a moment and Megan had the feeling that, like her, he was still working to control himself and whatever it was he was dealing with in the aftermath of her abrupt ending.

Then, sounding reluctant but resigned, he said, "Probably be better if we got out of the air before it does any more damage."

The same damage that was being done by remaining in his arms, by the continuing warmth of his breath in her hair, by having the rock-solid magnificence of his body all around her. The damage that could be done by giving in to the temptation to tell him she hadn't meant it when she'd told him to stop, to say *never mind, just go back to what you were doing*....

"It probably would be better if we got out of the night air," she agreed in a voice without much conviction.

Yet neither of them moved even then. Instead they stayed the way they were, entwined, their clothes askew and bare flesh still pressed to bare flesh in a way that felt so right...

And if ever there had been anything in her life more difficult than pushing away from him, Megan didn't know what it was.

But she knew she had to do it now or she never would, so she tilted her chin to kiss his Adam's apple and then drew back, doing her best to rearrange her bra and sweater as she did.

This time it was Josh who took a long, deep pull of air and sighed it out before he refastened the buttons on his own shirt.

Neither of them said anything then. Or as they walked back to his car. Or on the drive to her house.

And when Josh pulled to a stop in front of it Megan opened the passenger door before he could even think about turning off the engine and got out rather than risk a good-night kiss that she might not have the where-withal to end tonight.

But he wouldn't let her go that easily.

He rolled down his window and called to her just as she reached the porch steps, and Megan had to turn to face him again.

"It's a good thing you didn't want an apology because I'm not sorry," he said.

"I only wish I was," Megan answered in a voice that was barely above a whisper before she turned back around and ran for the house.

And it was true, she *did* wish she were sorry about what they'd shared just moments earlier.

If she had been maybe it wouldn't have been so difficult to leave him behind.

And maybe she wouldn't have had to take with her such a fierce craving for more of it that she couldn't get comfortable in her own bed.

Chapter 9

MEGAN SPENT FRIDAY AT her office. Annissa had gone to Denver to see an old friend and wouldn't be back until late Sunday so Megan needed to man the fort. Which wasn't bad because besides answering the phone to schedule appointments for them both, she also had two acupuncture clients drop in for treatments.

It didn't make for a rushed and harried day but she was busy most of it. Busy enough so that she could have—*should* have—not spent it thinking about Josh almost every minute. Wondering where he was. What he was doing. If he might call or come by at any moment. Wishing he would.

Of course she told herself she was worried about what he might be doing in regards to the investigation and in pursuit of her parents. But deep down she knew that wasn't the real reason he was on her mind.

The real reason was that somehow, in the short time she'd known him, something had happened and now it was as if he were a part of her every thought, her every breath, her every heartbeat.

She didn't want that to be the case and she tried to

deny it, but that day was evidence of just how true it was because even though he wasn't with her in body, he was still with her in spirit. Each detail of his jaw-droppingly handsome face was an intriguing picture in her mind's eye. His dark bourbon voice was an imaginary whisper in her ear. His lips seemed to have left a permanent imprint on hers. And having his arms around her, his hands on her body the way they'd been the night before? That was a nearly overwhelming craving that kept sneaking up on her when she least expected it.

Like as dusk was falling and she was ready to close the office. That craving hit her again, pushing her to go home by way of the courthouse, to drop in on him.

She had the perfect excuse. She could say she just wanted to know what he'd been up to all day and if he'd found out anything more that took suspicions off her parents.

But that's all it would be—an excuse—because what she was really after was seeing Josh himself.

She knew it would do her good to go a full day and night without that. That it might even help get him out of her system if she didn't have yet another evening with him inflaming her already intense attraction to him. But it didn't help curb that craving once it began.

She was still sitting behind her desk, arguing with herself about what to do when the phone rang. Yes, her first thought and her greatest—if unbidden—hope was that it would be Josh on the other end of the line.

But that wasn't who it was.

It was her mother's voice, sounding only slightly less

distant and diffused than her father's had when they'd spoken days before.

"Is that you, Megan?"

"Yes, it's me," she confirmed. "I'm so glad you called! Is the weather better there?"

"It's still raining but not the way it was when your dad talked to you. He said he promised that we'd get back to you, though, so I thought I'd try again now that the storm isn't completely raging."

"Did he tell you what's going on?" Megan asked, needing to raise her voice to make sure it was heard over the static that was still in the background of this call the way it had been in the other one.

"He told me what you told him."

Megan was grateful that she didn't have to fill her mother in and use their time rehashing what she'd already gone over with her father.

"I don't know how long I'll be able to talk," her mother said then. "I'm on a ship-to-shore and you're conferenced in from there, and the weather is still interfering."

"I'll get right to it, then. You guys need to get hold of the sheriff here so he can interview you. Let me give you his name and number right off the bat in case we get cut off."

Megan did just that, surprised that merely saying Josh's name was enough to set off a flutter in the pit of her stomach.

But she tried to ignore it and when she'd given her mother Josh's information, she said, "I have to warn you, he's very interested in why you didn't sell out when you left Elk Creek and where you got the money to travel since you didn't."

"We didn't have all that much money. We'd been saving since we decided to go and we just figured that when that ran out we'd work along the way."

"That's what I thought. I told him you probably didn't sell the farm because you wanted it to stay in the family."

"That's why, yes. But even if we'd wanted to sell we couldn't have. Real estate of any kind wasn't selling then and even people who tried to find buyers weren't having any luck."

"Was there anyone in particular financial trouble that you know of?"

"Well…" her mother said, clearly thinking about that. "There were the Brownwells down the road. Their cattle contracted some kind of virus and most of the animals had to be destroyed, which nearly wiped them out, as I recall. And there were the Shaunesseys. They'd been struggling for a long time and when they finally decided to give up and sell, they couldn't. Their place was still on the market when we left and they were picking up work around town, doing whatever anyone would pay them to do to get by. I know that their problems finding a buyer caused the Murphys next door to come to us when they wanted to sell out and ask if we might be interested in expanding our place. But I don't think they were having money trouble so much as that they'd just gotten too old to work that hard anymore."

"I haven't heard of any Brownwells or Shaunesseys but Mabel Murphy is still here."

"No? She's alive? She must be ancient by now." The static seemed to be getting worse but the call wasn't breaking up the way so much of the one from her father had.

"Mabel is pretty old," Megan told her mother. "She's spry, though. Her husband died a few years ago and she lives there alone, but she seems to do pretty well by herself. The house needs paint and some repairs but she's cooking and cleaning and baking and getting around under her own steam."

"Good for her!"

"Maybe they just quit working their place and decided to stay after all."

"Maybe. And maybe you and Nissa should see if you could paint or do some repairs if she needs it now. She was always good to you girls."

"I thought about that. Oh, and I forgot to tell Dad that Mabel still has that hall tree he made for her. She hides her love letters in it."

A burst of static cut off her mother's laughter and assaulted Megan's ear, preventing her from hearing anything for a moment.

When it had died down some, Megan said, "Did either you or Dad remember anything else about Pete Chaney that might get you off the hook here?"

"We've talked about it and talked about it since your dad called you, but there just isn't anything else to say. Pete worked for us for a while and, as far as I know, left when we did."

More static sounded, lasting longer this time than the last.

"Sounds like we're going to lose this connection, honey," her mother said, having to nearly shout. "Before we do, tell me how you and Nissa are doing."

"We're fine," Megan yelled in return. "Nissa's getting in a few more clients than I am right now but I think it will even out once word gets around." Which reminded her that she had yet another reason to talk to Josh—to see if his acupuncture had worked. "How about you and Dad? Is everything okay?"

"Last night we flashed floodlights on a midnight dumping of solvents from another ship. Stopped them cold. It was wonderful!" The excitement in her mother's voice was audible even over the static. But then she said, "I'm going to have to hang up, Megan. Tell your sheriff we'll get to him when we can and—"

The line went dead just then and after calling for her mother several times to make sure she really was gone, Megan hung up.

She sat for a moment with the thought that she now had a genuine reason to stop by Josh's office—she needed to report her mother's phone call to him.

Not that she couldn't do that over the phone, which would avoid the risks that were inherent in being with him.

But she knew she wasn't just going to call him. That she wasn't going to do anything that kept her from seeing him in the flesh. So to speak.

So she stood and pushed her chair in, resigned to her own weakness when it came to the man and wondering if it was the same kind of weakness her parents had for each other or the same kind of weakness that kept Mabel Murphy hiding old love letters in the hall tree.

For some reason once the image of the hall tree was in her mind she couldn't shake it. It seemed to niggle at her.

Strange, she thought, not understanding it.

Then her conversation with her mother popped into her thoughts, too, and it all felt like pieces of a puzzle that were important even though she wasn't sure how they fit together.

Until, out of the blue, she recalled something else. Something that made several things fall into place all of a sudden.

"Oh, no. Don't make this be how it was," she lamented as if she weren't alone in the office.

But the longer she thought about it, the more convinced she was that she knew who had buried Pete Chaney in her backyard.

And as much as she wanted to see Josh, seeing him under *these* circumstances was not at all what she'd had in mind.

"Are you going to tell me yet why we're here?" Josh asked as they got out of their respective cars half an hour later.

Megan had gone by his office and requested that he follow her but she hadn't told him why. She hadn't told him anything at all. She hadn't wanted to do much talking one way or another as she mulled what was on her mind.

"I'm hoping there are some reasonable explanations,"

was her only answer to Josh's question about why they were where they were as they climbed the porch steps of the paint-peeled farmhouse where lights shone through the living room window like welcoming beacons.

Welcoming beacons that made Megan feel worse.

She rang the doorbell, waiting without looking at Josh standing tall and straight beside her because she didn't want to be distracted by him and she knew just one glance would do that.

Mabel Murphy opened the door without asking who was there and smiled cheerily when she recognized them.

"What a nice surprise!" she said.

"Can we talk to you?" Megan asked by way of greeting, the serious tone of her voice giving away the fact that she wasn't on a social call.

Mabel's expression sobered. "Of course," she said somewhat more formally as she stepped aside to allow them in.

The house was as warm and inviting as it had been when they'd been there before and for a moment Megan considered keeping the conclusion she'd come to to herself.

If it hadn't been her own parents who would be left in jeopardy if she did, that's exactly what she might have done. But as it was she let Mabel lead them into the living room, shoring up her courage along the way.

The elderly woman turned off the television that was blaring with a game show, and into the silence that followed, she said, "Can I get you both something to drink? Coffee? Tea? A glass of wine?"

Josh and Megan declined the offer and it occurred to Megan that Josh was unusually subdued, taking the role of observer until he knew exactly what was going on.

"What did you want to talk about?" Mabel asked then, settling into her overstuffed lounger as Megan and Josh sat on the couch—Megan on the very edge of the cushion as if she didn't have the right to be more comfortable than that.

"I spoke to my mother just a little while ago and some things she told me started me to thinking," Megan began.

She told both Mabel and Josh about her conversation with her mother, about learning that some of Elk Creek's residents had been in financial trouble when her family had left town but had been unable to sell their property even when they needed to. That the Murphys in particular had wanted her family to buy them out.

"My folks just thought that you and Mr. Murphy had reached a time in your life when you didn't want to work as hard as you needed to to keep the place going. But after I got off the phone I started wondering if maybe that wasn't true. If maybe you'd been in financial trouble, too."

Megan waited and watched Mabel. But the elderly woman's expression was perfectly calm.

Hoping she was wrong in what she was thinking, Megan continued.

"Then I remembered something else. Two things, actually. I remembered that the man who'd sold the gold doubloons in Cheyenne eighteen years ago had been an older man with a limp, and I remembered you showing us the hall tree my dad had carved for you, that antique umbrellas weren't the only things you kept in it."

Megan pointed to the seated hall tree that was visible through the archway to the living room. "I recalled also seeing walking sticks in it. And then it occurred to me that walking sticks and canes are basically the same thing. And that canes are used by people with limps."

Megan felt rather than saw Josh's interest pique at that.

"You don't need any help getting around," Megan observed. "So when I saw the walking sticks—the canes—earlier, I assumed you just collected them. But now I'm wondering if Mr. Murphy needed them."

Mabel took a deep breath that raised her frail shoulders and lowered them again when she sighed it out. Then she smiled. Still perfectly calmly. As if she'd been waiting for this to happen for a long while and was well-prepared.

"Horace fell from the barn loft the year before that year you're so interested in. Broke his hip. We hadn't been doing well financially for a few years so we'd dropped our medical insurance coverage and without it we couldn't afford the hip replacement surgery he should have had. The hip just had to heal and it left him with a limp. He also ended up not bein' able to work the place the way he had. Which left us in very hard times."

"And you were going to lose everything when along came Pete Chaney and his gold doubloons," Megan guessed.

"Yep. But it wasn't what you're thinkin'. Pete Chaney

came by here after you and your folks left town. Offered to work in exchange for food and sleepin' in our barn. We had some things needed doin' that Horace couldn't take care of, thought maybe if we spruced up the place we'd have a better chance of finding a buyer before the bank left us with nothin'. So we made the deal with Chaney and set him up in the tack room. Next morning Horace went lookin' for him when he didn't show up for breakfast and there he was, dead in his bunk. Must have had a heart attack or a stroke or something while he slept."

"Nothing that would show up in what was left of his remains eighteen years later," Megan pointed out for Josh's benefit, refraining from gloating over the fact that that's what she'd suggested at the start of this.

"We'd heard—same as everybody had—Chaney's stories about the gold coins he claimed to have," Mabel continued. "Nobody—us included—believed he had any such thing. But after Horace found 'im, we went through his knapsack and, sure enough, he had two gold doubloons. So there we were, faced with a man who'd died of natural causes, who'd just told us how he was all alone in the world, how he didn't have a single bit of kinfolk, and us with two gold doubloons in hand and the bank barkin' at the back door. What would you have done?"

But Mabel didn't wait for an answer to that before she went on. "Not a soul in town would've—or did—think a thing about a drifter being here one day and not the next. If we'd of called the sheriff he'd have taken the coins, used 'em to bury the man and who knows what would have happened with anything left over. And we'd of still lost our home. So we decided there was no harm doin' the burying ourselves and keepin' the coins for our trouble."

Simple enough.

"But why bury him in my family's backyard?" Megan asked.

Mabel shrugged. "We were afraid of buryin' him here. Afraid if he got dug up somehow nobody'd believe we didn't kill him. It didn't seem like your family'd ever come back or that anybody'd be able to track 'em down if the body showed up on their property. So we took Chaney over to your place late that night and dug him a grave there."

"And then your husband took the coins into Cheyenne, sold them, and that's how you saved the farm," Megan concluded unnecessarily.

"That's the whole of it."

"Why not just keep the coins no one believed Chaney had in the first place and call the sheriff to report the death?" Josh asked then, sounding slightly more conversational than officious, which helped ease some of Megan's fears for Mabel.

"We knew we'd have to sell 'em," the older woman said matter-of-factly. "And when we did, if word got out somehow, it'd be easy to figure that we took them off of Chaney and someone might take the money away from us. But doin' it the way we did—with Horace using Chaney's name when he sold them—if word got out, folks would just think he'd sold them himself after leavin' here and nobody'd be the wiser."

"And the bank didn't question where you'd all of a sudden come up with the money to pay them?" This from Josh.

"It wasn't like we walked in and plunked down enough to pay off the mortgage—although we could have. We just caught up on the payments and went on making them from there as if we didn't have a whole lot of cash we were diggin' into."

Mabel took another deep breath, apparently signaling that her story was over. Then she said, "So, Josh, go ahead and arrest me if that's what you have to do."

This time Megan did turn her head to look at him.

Josh's eyes went from her to Mabel in a slow pivot as he seemed to ponder what had just been laid out before him.

Then, after a long moment, he said, "I'm obligated to write this up and talk to the District Attorney but I don't know what action he could take. There's no evidence that what you're saying isn't true, and, beyond unlawful disposal of human remains, I don't know where taking the coins stands. But no matter what it might qualify as, the statute of limitations has likely expired on that. So no, I'm not taking you in. But you sure could have saved me some time tellin' me this when we were here before."

Since Mabel hadn't shown any signs of alarm from the beginning, she didn't seem relieved to hear that she wasn't under arrest. All she said was, "I'm sorry for that. But I didn't know where I stood and I thought I was better off not tellin' something that might never come out at all."

Josh shook his head again, returning his midnight-blue eyes to Megan. "And you. You could have told me what you'd found out before we got here."

"I didn't want you barreling in here and doing something harsh if I was wrong."

"Oh right, because I'm known for being harsh with little old ladies. Pardon me callin' you that, Mabel," he added without looking at the elderly woman.

Then his gaze went back and forth between them as something else seemed to occur to him. "The two of you didn't cook this up to get your parents off the hook, did you?"

"I beg your pardon," Megan said.

"I still have the paperwork for the sale of the coins if you'd like to see it," Mabel offered in Megan's defense.

"I'll definitely need that," Josh said, still looking at Megan while Mabel got up and went to a rolltop desk in the corner of the living room.

From there she produced a yellowed paper Megan could only assume verified the sale of the gold doubloons when the elderly woman handed it to Josh.

He finally glanced away, reading what was written on the paper.

When he was finished he looked to Megan again. "Okay, so you're just good at playing Nancy Drew and you didn't concoct this whole thing."

He refolded the paper and put it in his breast pocket, getting to his feet as he did. "Well, Mabel, you never fail to amaze me."

"This was a trick I wished I didn't have to have up

my sleeve," she said. "But it was all that saved us back then."

Josh nodded, solemnly but with a resigned sort of understanding. "I'll get back to you with what the DA has to say."

"It's all right if you have to arrest me. I won't hold it against you."

"Good. But don't pack your toothbrush just yet."

Megan had stood, too, and she couldn't help apologizing to Mabel for having to reveal the long-kept secret. "If it hadn't been for my parents—"

"Don't fret about it," Mabel said as she stood, too, to walk them to the door. "What was done was done. I wouldn't have let it get so far that your folks had to answer for it."

Megan believed that but she still felt guilty for having had to be the one to air the elderly woman's dirty laundry.

"It'd be nice if word didn't have to get out around town, though," Mabel commented pointedly as they went into the entryway.

"I'll do what I can," Josh said. "Can't say I'd be thrilled myself if news spread that the acupuncturist here solved my first big case before I did. But I can't control what comes from the DA."

"I guess we'll just let the cards fall where they may," Mabel said. Then, in an aside to Josh, she added, "But you might try some sweet-talk with Megan to keep her quiet."

They all laughed at that and exchanged good-nights. Then Megan and Josh went back outside.

As they retraced their path down the porch steps to the waiting cars it finally sank in for Megan that her parents were free and clear of any criminal charges. And that, coupled with the likelihood that there also wouldn't be any repercussions for her neighbor, made her feel an enormous relief.

"This all must have been bothering me even more than I thought. I suddenly feel as if a weight has been lifted from my shoulders," she confided.

"I have to admit I'm glad it didn't turn out to be your folks. Even though I spent all day today finding out how to go about getting them back here, I wasn't happy to have to do it."

"Do you think it'll be all right for Mabel?"

"I wouldn't have told her so if I didn't."

They'd reached Megan's car by then and it struck her like a thunderbolt that they'd just lost any excuse for seeing each other. That for all intents and purposes there was no reason not to say *see you around sometime* and go their separate ways. Forever.

But Megan didn't say it and her stomach clenched at the thought that Josh might.

Then, before she even knew she was going to make the suggestion, she said, "I think we should celebrate."

"Well, it *is* Friday night," he agreed, welcoming the idea with enough enthusiasm to make her think he'd been as reluctant as she was to have their being together end so abruptly. "The Buckin' Bronco has dancing to a live band. Will that do?"

Anything would do as long as it meant she wasn't

VICTORIA PADE

207

suddenly faced with saying goodbye to him. "Sounds like fun."

"I need to shower and change clothes. How 'bout I pick you up in half an hour?"

"Make it an hour so I can shower and change, too."

"You got it."

Josh went on standing there a moment longer. And it occurred to Megan as she watched his expression that he knew—just as she did—that despite the fact that she'd superficially tied this evening to the tail-end of the investigation, the truth was, if they spent tonight together there was only one reason for it. And that reason was that they *wanted* to spend tonight together.

But neither of them mentioned that.

And although Megan had no idea what was going to happen once this evening was over, she gave herself permission to have these next few hours free of all the shoulds and shouldn'ts she'd struggled with since meeting this man. The specter of something bad happening to her parents had been lifted and she was just going to let herself enjoy that fact without a care in the world.

She was just going to let herself enjoy what would likely be her last night with Josh....

Chapter 10

MEGAN WORE THE *TAKE-ME* DRESS. That's what Nissa
called it, anyway.

It was a black slip dress with spaghetti straps. That's
all there was to it. One slinky length of fine silk that
fell in curve-kissing perfection to just above her knees.
She'd bought it with her honeymoon in mind then hadn't
had the honeymoon and so had never worn it.

But tonight she just had to break out the black
dress.

She knew that if Nissa were there her sister would tell
her she was just asking for trouble. That it was hardly
honky-tonk attire. That it really was a *take-me* dress and
that she might as well just meet the man at the door in
her birthday suit.

But Josh had only seen her in jeans or in dresses Noel
had said belonged in a schoolyard. And tonight that
wasn't the impression she wanted to give. If this was
the last concentrated time they ever spent together, she
wanted to leave him with just one knock-out vision of
her.

So she'd opted for the slip dress. And a pair of three-

inch-high heels that were held on her feet by nothing
more than a single strap across the top of each foot.

She left her hair straight after shampooing it, letting
it hang loose around shoulders she dusted with glitter.
Then she applied a little blush and a bit more mascara
than usual, and judged herself ready for a night of celebrating.

She was ready to go and waiting at the living room
window when Josh pulled up in the squad car. That was
all it took to make her heart beat double-time and for
butterflies to take flight in her stomach. But tonight, she
decided, the same way she wasn't going to torment herself with shoulds and shouldn'ts, she also wasn't going
to fight what seeing him, being with him, did to her.
Tonight they were two people out on a date, celebrating,
and she was going to go with the flow.

In keeping with that, when Josh did get out of the
car, Megan allowed herself to feast openly on the sight
of him.

He was dressed in cowboy boots and black jeans that
fit him just snugly enough to hint at the glory of his tight
derriere and immense thighs without being so tight they
looked as if he'd been poured into them.

Gone was the uniform shirt and in its place was a
bright red Western shirt with a black collar, cuffs and
placket. It was fitted so that it rode his broad shoulders
and chest and then hugged his narrow waist. And maybe
Megan was only projecting her own thoughts onto him,
but she had the impression that that shirt said that he
was cutting loose tonight, too.

She left the window and went to the door to open it

before he had the chance to ring the bell. Although she wasn't sure if he'd intended to because Josh already had the screen open when she did.

"Wow!" he said with one look at her. And if eyes really could pop out she thought his might have.

Mission accomplished.

"You approve?" she asked with a smile she couldn't suppress.

"Holy cow, you look incredible."

"Thank you," she said as if it didn't thrill her to her toes to see how stunned he was. "You look pretty good yourself."

And he smelled wonderful, too, as he stepped inside and the scent of his aftershave wafted all around her.

"Am I really going to have to share you with a bar full of other guys?" he asked then.

"Celebration dancing—that's what you promised and I'm going to hold you to it."

"I'd like to be held to you," he muttered under his breath.

The comment and the way his eyes were devouring her tempted her to consider agreeing to cancel their plans and make some entirely new ones that didn't involve leaving home. But wearing the *take-me* dress was as daring as she was ready to be, so she said, "Uh-uh. Dancing at the Buckin' Bronco. That was the deal."

"Then tell me you'll only dance with me," he ordered.

"I'll only dance with you," she complied perfunctorily to conceal the fact that she didn't have any inclination whatsoever to dance with anyone else.

"This is still going to be tough on me," he said with yet another glance that ran her up and down.

"You've been tough on me all week," Megan countered.

"All I did was suspect your parents of murder," he said as if it were no big deal. "But you lookin' like that and gettin' my blood boiling when we have to be out in public—that's more payback than I deserve."

Megan just gave him a Cheshire cat smile and handed him the matching shawl wrap that went with the dress.

Josh draped it around her shoulders but once he had he kept his hands on them for a moment before he took them away and sighed. "Oh, yeah, this is way more payback than I deserve," he said as he held the door open for her and ushered her to his car.

On the way into town Josh let her know that he'd gotten hold of an assistant district attorney who had confirmed that there wasn't anything to charge Mabel Murphy with and that beyond filing a report, the matter would be closed.

Megan told him how happy she was to hear that and that she'd left a message for her parents telling them they'd been cleared.

"So that's it for the whole thing," Josh concluded. "Which means that the rest of tonight can just be about having fun."

"Agreed," Megan said as he pulled into the parking lot of the Buckin' Bronco.

And that really was the end of any talk about Pete Chaney and what had happened to him. Not that they could have discussed it further even if they'd wanted to because once they stepped inside the honky tonk the noise of the band and the crowd made it impossible for any kind of actual conversation.

Of course Josh knew just about everybody in the place but he got them a small table in one corner so no one could join them. Then he ordered a bottle of champagne.

And between glasses of the bubbly stuff they spent the entire evening dancing line dances and two-steps and cowboy waltzes until Megan's head was light and her feet ached and she couldn't remember when she'd had a better time.

"Last call," the bartender shouted at a little before 2:00 a.m. and the band's lead singer countered with, "Last dance, too."

The place was only about half as full as it had been when Megan and Josh had arrived so when Josh led her out to the dance floor they had plenty of space. But by then Megan was accustomed to him swinging her into his arms and holding her close, and it didn't matter how much room they had to spread out, he still pulled her up against him with one hand at the small of her back and the other holding her hand between them.

They could have talked as they danced then because the song was slow and much softer than most of what had been played all evening. But neither of them did. It was just too nice to go on the way they had been, letting their bodies do the communicating as they did barely more than sway together, Megan's head on Josh's chest, Josh's cheek resting on her crown.

Then, out of the blue, Josh whispered, "I don't want this to be over."

"Neither do I," she admitted even though she wasn't exactly sure what he didn't want to be over, whether it was the dance or the evening or what they'd been playing at from the start. But it didn't matter. She didn't want any of it to end.

"What are we going to do about it?" he asked then.

"What do you want to do about it?"

He chuckled, a husky rumble she wouldn't have been able to hear if her ear hadn't been pressed to him. "I want to take you home and make love to you," he said just as quietly.

Megan smiled against him. Maybe it was all the champagne or all the dancing. Maybe it was all the feelings she had for this man that had been growing secretly since the moment they'd met. Or maybe it was that she'd been taught that desire was a natural thing and that nothing nature designed was bad. But unlike the night before, she was no longer thinking about the fact that they were two very different people. She wasn't thinking about how much she'd been hurt by those differences and her former fiancé's attempts to change her. She wasn't thinking about how much she might be hurt by Josh if she got in any deeper than she already was.

Tonight she was only thinking about the possibility that this could be her last chance with Josh. Her last chance to have those natural—and very intense—desires fulfilled.

Tonight she was only thinking that, come what may, she didn't want to pass up that chance.

So she heard herself say, "Nissa is gone for the night."

Josh lifted his head from the top of hers and craned to look into her face.

He was smiling a small, tentative smile that said he still wasn't ready to rush into anything.

"Careful what you're saying, darlin', because I meant what I said about makin' love to you."

And he didn't want to get near to that and have her stop things the way she had the night before. The night before when she'd said she didn't want them to go too far and he'd honored that request.

But the night before hadn't seemed like her last chance....

"I know," she said quietly, raising her head from his chest to look into those navy-blue eyes of his.

"You're sure?"

Megan nodded but Josh still wasn't in any hurry. Instead he searched her expression as if to make certain she knew what she was getting into.

But she didn't have any doubts so she was confident he wouldn't find any of them in her face and she merely waited for him to convince himself.

Which was just what he must have done because when the song ended and the singer had bid the room sweet dreams, Josh kept hold of her hand to return to their table only to snatch up her shawl and take her out to his car.

Luckily it was a short drive to her place. And once they were there he wasted no time helping her out of the car and taking her up the porch steps.

"You're sure?" he repeated as she unlocked the front door.

Megan glanced over her shoulder at him and smiled without comment. She was sure. Sure she wanted him more than she'd ever wanted anything or anyone in her life.

Then she led him inside. Into the dark entryway. And as if that seclusion was all they'd been waiting for, Josh spun her around just enough to scoop her into his arms to carry her up the stairs to her room.

But he didn't take her all the way to the bed.

He stopped a few feet away from it and set her on her feet.

Moonlight was the only illumination they had but it was enough to drench them both in a milky glow, to allow them to see each other.

For a moment Josh stared down into her face again, delving into her eyes with his.

"I'm out of my mind over you," he whispered as he bent far enough forward to kiss the side of her neck.

Megan could only smile once more and let her head fall back to free the way for him to press his lips to the hollow of her throat, then to the other side of her neck before he reached her mouth with his.

The kiss was slow and sweet, lingering like a summer breeze in a sycamore tree until he ended it to kiss her cheekbones, one right after the other. Then he kissed the bridge of her nose, too. And her brow, smiling against her skin before he found her mouth once more.

His big hands gently bracketed her neck, his thumbs reaching up past her jaws to stroke her face so lightly it was the brush of angel's wings as his lips parted over hers, as he drew only her lower lip between his, and then only her upper lip.

He was toying with her but with a sensuality so potent it seeped into her pores and lit a fire in her stomach that spread fingers of arousal up to her breasts and down to that much lower spot of her body that ached with an enduring curiosity to know him in the most intimate sense.

But it was much too early yet for that and so instead she just gave herself over to his mouth on hers. To lips parted and urging hers to part, too. To his playful tongue when it came to greet hers.

She did lay her hands on his chest, though, indulging in the brick-wall hardness of that arousal that was gaining ground with each passing moment began to niggle at her, urging her on to more.

As their mouths went on exploring, meeting, parting, as their tongues teased and toyed, she searched for and found the top button of his shirt, unfastening it and moving down to the rest until she came up against the waistband of his jeans. Then she pulled the tails free and laid her palms flat against his washboard belly this time.

Up or down? an impish little voice in the back of her mind asked.

Oh, how she wanted to go down!

But she wasn't that brave. Yet. So instead she went up. Sliding along his skin, rising to honed pectorals where his nipples were only a fraction as hard as hers were.

And hers *were* hard. So hard she thought they might burst right through the silk confines of her dress.

But Josh didn't leave her wanting for long. One hand slid from the side of her face, down her neck to the spaghetti strap that slipped off her shoulder without too much encouragement and took part of the dress with it so that the uppermost curve of her breast was exposed to the air and just the faintest stroke of Josh's fingertips.

She stood a little straighter. Not intentionally, but in answer to the overpowering need for more than that.

Josh obliged, taking her whole breast in his hand, and even though her dress still stood between them, it felt good enough for a tiny moan to echo in her throat.

Then he inched the dress farther down on that same side, freeing her at last to the warm kid-leather of his palm where her nipple fitted as perfectly as if it had been carved from it.

Kneading, caressing, teasing…

Arousal was turning to flames that licked her insides with hotter need than she'd ever known. So hot she kicked off her shoes as if that would help cool her off and let her hands slide over Josh's shoulders until his shirt fell around their feet and she could press her own palms to his bare flesh.

He did a bit of a two-step himself to get his boots off and she knew he was as driven as she was because he was breathing so deeply that massive chest of his rose beneath her searching hands.

Then he slipped her other strap down and that was all it took for the whole dress to fall in a gossamer wisp around her ankles, leaving her with only nylons to dispose of—something he did without hesitation, leaving her naked before him.

That was when his mouth deserted hers so he could look at her. Openly. As if she were a work of art.

And as he did he slipped out of what remained of his clothes.

Megan felt a flash of self-consciousness but she forgot all about that the moment she could feast on the sight of him. There was no better word to describe him than magnificent. Sleek and muscular and perfectly proportioned, it occurred to her that it was a crime to ever cover him up with clothes.

And he wanted her. That was more than evident.

He took her into his arms again, capturing her mouth once more with his, enclosing her breast in the warm grip of his hand, his desire for her nestled between them.

Then he took her the rest of the way to the bed, lying them down on their sides, facing each other. One of his arms was her pillow while he wrapped the other around her and pulled her closer, rubbing her back as he went on kissing her, plundering her mouth with his probing tongue in hungry abandon now.

His leg came over hers and once more she could feel the intensity of his desire for her against the lowest part of her pubic bone, long and hard and strong. And this time when that little voice in the back of her mind urged her downward she complied, encompassing that length and strength in her hand.

He groaned a groan that almost sounded like agony. But she knew it was an agony of pleasure as she explored him, learned the wonders of that staff that was as magnificent as the rest of him.

Then he rolled her to her back, still kissing her, his mouth open wide, his tongue mastering hers before he began two descents of his own.

His hand trailed a caressing stroke to her stomach as he kissed his way to her abandoned breast, taking her nipple into the wonderful dark mystery of his mouth, teasing, tugging with his teeth, sucking it deeply in and flicking that incredibly sensitive crest with the tip of his tongue.

Then his hand went farther still, finding its way between her thighs, slipping his finger into that center of her that had wanted him from the very beginning.

But by then Megan was nearly wild with desire, with yearning, with need. Her spine arched all on its own, pulling her up off the bed as if she were riding an ocean wave.

Josh got the message. He tore his mouth from her breast and rose above her, fitting himself between her thighs and coming inside her in one fluid motion, embedding himself into her, claiming her, making her his.

He drew out of her, slowly, slowly and so far that for one awful moment Megan thought he might pull free and steal from her the wonder of that stupendous body filling her the way her body was screaming to be filled.

But just as she was about to protest he plunged back in, even farther than he'd been before, so far that her spine arched a second time and her shoulders left the bed again, thrusting her breasts impudently into his chest.

Josh insinuated his hand underneath her then and, making sure to hold her firmly enough to him that they didn't part, he rolled them both to their sides again.

Once they were there his mouth recaptured hers in a wide-open, hungry play of lips and teeth and tongues as his talented hand returned to her engorged breast, to the nipple that was so taut it was like a tiny granite pebble against his palm.

He held her hips to him with one powerful leg thrown over them as he moved deeply into her yet again. In and out. Choreographing a perfect dance, a perfect union of pleasure, of passion as every sense played its part.

But that passion mounted and mounted until Megan's head fell away from their kiss. Until Josh's hand abandoned her breast so he could hold her tightly against him as he took total control, as he pushed into her so completely it felt as if he were reaching the core of her. Again. Again.

Each thrust took Megan a step closer to what she was striving for. To what she needed with increasing desperation. Higher. Faster. Harder. Straining to break free of the constraints of anything that bound her beyond the bliss that Josh alone could provide. Joining her to him body and soul, shooting them both through to the heavens.

They clung to each other, melded into one in that single, pure instant of ecstasy when Megan needed nothing so much as Josh all around her, inside her. As something she didn't even know she was capable of exploded in a white-hot glory that caught her breath and held her suspended in something so blissful, so profound, that she wasn't sure she would survive...

But of course she did.

And when it was over, when both she and Josh came floating back to earth, Megan couldn't help wondering how she had ever lived without knowing such flawless rapture before.

How she could go on if she never knew it again...

But as she caught her breath she reminded herself that she still had that moment. That moment with Josh in her bed. Lying in his arms. And she didn't want to spoil it by thinking about anything that had come before making love with him. Or anything that might come later.

She just wanted to go on reveling in what she had right then.

And so, when he slipped out of her and settled her beside him, her head on his chest, she let herself slide into replete sleep, telling herself that she would deal with whatever came tomorrow when tomorrow came.

Chapter 11

JOSH SLEPT LATER THE next morning than he had since he was a teenager. And when he woke up at nearly 10:00 a.m. he knew he should get right out of bed. He knew that, even though it was Saturday, he should go into the office to make some calls and close out the file on Pete Chaney and the Murphys.

But the bed he was in wasn't his own. It was Megan's. And she was asleep beside him, using his chest as her pillow, one of her legs slung over one of his thighs, her palm pressed to his shoulder, her breath soft and warm on his skin. Just the way she'd been when they'd fallen asleep after making love.

And he certainly had no desire to disturb anything.

Especially not when he wasn't sure where things between them would go from here.

He was very much aware that he hadn't gone a day without seeing her since they'd met. And last night, after Megan had solved the Pete Chaney case and just before she'd suggested they celebrate, he'd been wondering how he was going to keep on seeing her without the excuse of the investigation.

And now there he was, in her bed, back to wondering what would happen.

Wondering what would happen and knowing that the one thing he *didn't* want was to stop seeing her.

Stop seeing her? That was an understatement. He didn't want to spend five minutes away from her. Ever.

He didn't completely understand it but there was something about having made love to her that had lowered the wall of self-delusion he'd been fortifying from the moment he'd first laid eyes on her. The wall of self-delusion that had led him to believe that while he might be attracted to Megan, he could keep himself from going any further than that. That he could keep himself from getting involved with her. From having feelings for her. From falling head-over-heels for her.

But self-delusion was really all that had been. And making love to her had shone a great big spotlight on the truth.

The truth that he was most definitely involved with her. That he had feelings for her. Deep feelings that put him smack dab in the middle of being head-over-heels for her. That made him want never to let her go.

But wasn't he jumping from the pan into the fire with yet another mercurial woman? She was an acupuncturist, for crying out loud. She arranged her furniture according to Feng shui and hung crystals in corners. And by no stretch of the imagination had she led an ordinary life or been raised by run-of-the-mill people. All of which seemed like warnings to him that he might be on the same path he'd been on with Farrah. A path of destruction.

He reminded himself that after Farrah he'd sworn that he would never have anything to do with another flaky, flighty woman. He'd learned his lesson—flaky and flighty translated into irresponsible and unreliable.

Off-the-wall women—and Megan qualified as *that*—couldn't be trusted. They were too capricious. Too fickle. Too unstable. And he'd vowed that there was no way he was ever going to give his heart to another woman like that.

Yet there he was with his heart on his sleeve, ready to hand it over to Megan.

But as he looked down at her sleeping so peacefully, he started to actually think about the kind of person she was. To separate her from the acupuncture and the Feng shui and the crystals and all the rest of that odd stuff she embraced.

Yes, the trappings were, in his opinion, as weird as Farrah's interests in all things metaphysical. But Megan didn't base her decisions on any kind of metaphysical dictates. Well, okay, she based her decision of where to put her furniture on something not too far removed from it, but guidance in where to put a couch was hardly in a league with leaving him at the altar because a psychic had said to.

Megan the person was very different from Farrah. Megan had strong family values. Just like he did. She had the same goals he did—settling in Elk Creek, putting down roots, getting married and having kids. She was responsible. Loyal. Considerate. Caring. He'd seen all of that in her response to Mabel. In her defense of her parents.

Megan just wasn't the norm for Elk Creek.

So what if she *was* somewhat unorthodox? he asked himself. Was that so bad?

Okay, he'd thought the same thing about Farrah. But while Megan might be unorthodox she wasn't undependable or fickle or self-centered or downright unbalanced—all the things Farrah had proven to be.

Instead, Megan was interesting and unique. Not to mention smart and beautiful and funny and fun to be with and well-grounded and centered and sexy...

Oh yeah, so sexy she made his blood boil just by walking into a room.

And the bottom line, he realized as he held her even closer than he had been, was that whatever her views, whatever her background, whatever her occupation—and he had to admit that he hadn't had a single sneeze since her acupuncture treatment—he sure as hell didn't want to slip out of her bed and maybe out of her life.

He wanted to be with her every day. He wanted to build a life around her and have her life built around him. He wanted her to *be* his life.

Megan might not be like a lot of other women. She might not be what he'd thought he should be looking for.

But she wasn't Farrah, either.

And what she was, was everything he needed. Everything he wanted.

Wholeheartedly. From the depths of his soul. Without any doubt.

And ultimately wasn't that what mattered?

That and that she was someone he genuinely believed he could trust?

It was.

What mattered was that she was the person she was. What mattered was the way he felt about her.

And the way he felt about her was unique all on its own. It was like nothing he'd ever felt for anyone else. Farrah included.

And it was too strong to be denied for one minute longer.

Megan woke up to the feel of a feather-light tickle running from her shoulder to her wrist, from her wrist to her shoulder.

She knew instantly what it was, where she was and who she was snuggled up next to. And it made her smile against Josh's chest.

"That's a lot better than an alarm clock," she said, her voice quiet and sleepy but slightly husky, too, from the other things that he was awakening in her body at the same time he was rousing her from slumber.

"And it can be yours every morning for the rest of your life for just a small price," he said like an infomercial announcer.

"Mmm. That seems like a good deal," she countered, assuming he was kidding. "What's the small price?"

"You have to sleep with me every night for the rest of your life."

Megan laughed. "Wow, I must have really knocked your socks off last night. But I don't know if I could keep it up every night for the rest of my life," she joked again.

"Some nights we can just sleep. It's the *every* night that's the price."

Something in his voice told her he wasn't kidding at all and before she said anything else she opened her eyes to glance up at him.

Now *that* was something to wake up to every morning, she thought as she drank in the sight of him. His sharp jaw was stubbled with beard and while the scruffy look was not Megan's favorite, on Josh it was so incredibly sexy she was tempted to say anything to maintain the status quo.

But she had the sense that more was going on with him than she should disregard in favor of the pure sensual elements of waking up with him.

"*Every* night, huh?" she repeated quizzically.

"*Every* night," he confirmed.

"You aren't talking in your sleep, are you?"

"I'm wide awake. I have been for a while, lyin' here thinking."

"About what?"

"About how I want every morning to be just like this."

Every night. *Every* morning. And he seemed serious.

Megan held the sheet to her breasts with one hand and sat up in bed, curling her legs to one side underneath her.

When she did, Josh pushed himself up against the headboard, baring his glorious chest and distracting her until she forced herself not to look at it. Not to think about how good it had felt to lie against it.

"You're not just teasing, are you?" she surmised.

"Nope. Is that so bad?"

She wasn't sure. For some reason it didn't feel good. It made her sort of panicky.

"I don't know," she answered honestly. "I hadn't thought beyond last night." Last night when all she could think about was not having her time with him end...

"Well, think beyond it now," he commanded. "Would it be so horrible for us to be together as something more than partners in crime solving? I know it would mean meat in the refrigerator alongside the tofu and maybe a chair in front of the TV where it might block some of the energy flow or something, but I think we could work it out."

His tone when he talked about tofu and energy flow struck a sour note in Megan. She'd taken his comments about things like that before as simple skepticism, but they suddenly sounded disparaging to her. Worse than that, they also sounded like criticism. The same kind of criticism Noel had dished out behind veils of helpfulness and concern.

"I like the chairs where they are," she said stubbornly, the only concrete thing she could come up with.

"Okay, then we'll move the TV to the chairs. What I'm telling you is—"

"How I can change things to suit you."

That had come out more harshly than she'd meant for it to. But she was beginning to feel a little harsh. And defensive. And afraid. And disillusioned.

"I'm talking about compromise, is all," Josh said reasonably enough. "So we can be together."

"And what compromises would you make?"

He shrugged one broad shoulder and it occurred to Megan that he was causing her a terrible tug of war between what her head was telling her and the response her body had to nothing more than the knee-weakening sight of him. But this time she had to let her head rule. She *had* to.

"I'd make whatever compromises I'd need to," Josh said. "The point is, I know we're pretty different and I can't help thinkin' some of the things you're into are a little weird, but what I've come to realize is that *you're* not weird. That Megan Bailey the person is sweet and kind and compassionate and has the sort of character that makes her a decent person. That makes her everything I want. And since there's no question that I want you…"

Megan was holding up the sheet with only one hand and Josh took the other from where it rested in her lap, holding it gently as he continued.

"Since I want you so much it's like I'm under the influence of some magic spell, I'd really like it if we could work around the differences and be together."

In all he'd just said two things kept ringing in Megan's ears—that what she was interested in was *weird* to him, and that they were so different.

Too different, she couldn't help thinking. Too different if he considered anything about her weird.

She felt her head shaking before she was even sure why it was. Then she said, "No," with enough force to make Josh rear back slightly and look at her through shocked eyes.

"I know where this leads," she went on as her panic grew. "It starts here, it starts out nicely, but it ends with you trying to reshape me into something that fits the image you want me to be."

"No, it doesn't," he said, his handsome face sobering into a frown that looked on the verge of anger. Anger that echoed in his voice, too. "Compromise—that's all I'm talking about. People *have* to compromise to be together."

"Except I still haven't heard what *you're* going to do to compromise. I've only heard what you want *me* to do."

"Only because that's all that came off the top of my head."

"I know that's how it seems but the truth is, what comes off the top of anyone's head is very telling. Sure, meat in the fridge and a chair in front of the TV are small things but they're still things connected to me that you want changed. And this is only the beginning. Pretty soon there would be something else. Something bigger. And then something after that. And something after that. You've spent the whole time since the first day you walked into my office thinking I'm some kind of freak. And you told me yourself you wanted the tried and true. I know how one fits into the other and it doesn't involve you embracing the *weird* stuff I'm into, it involves you trying to show me just how weird it is and why it should be left by the wayside. It involves you trying to change me so I don't embarrass you."

"Farrah embarrassed me, you don't."

But Megan didn't believe him. She'd had too much experience with Noel, with a man who wanted something she wasn't and thought a few *compromises* on her part could give him that. She simply could not now feel confident that the same thing wouldn't happen with Josh. That before too long he wouldn't try to fit her into a mold that made him more comfortable.

She shook her head again. "We're too different, Josh."

"Deep down we *aren't* too different. That's part of what I realized when I started thinking about the two of us. We want the same kind of life in the same place. We enjoy each other. We're good together." He paused a moment, watching her with those midnight-blue eyes of his. "The differences between us are all just trappings. Outward stuff. Nothing that really matters."

"It all matters. It matters when you have some big dinner with the head of the sheriff's department and you worry that I might tell him what herb would help his psoriasis or that his wife's back problem could be helped by acupuncture because you think I'd sound like a nut. It matters when you take me to a barbecue at your friend's house and wish I'd eat the ribs he's cooking so I wouldn't seem rude. It's all small stuff, but it adds up. It all counts as the *weird*ness about me that you *don't* like. And what it adds up to is not wanting me to be me."

"You're who I'm crazy about. Why would I not want you to be you?"

"Because it will embarrass you because you don't believe in the same things I believe in. Because we're different and you don't want different—you told me so yourself."

"I want you," he said as if he knew it without a doubt.

But his certainty didn't override Megan's doubts. "It won't work," she decreed, feeling as if her heart were breaking even as she did.

"How do you know it won't work until we try?"

"I know. I've been there."

"You haven't been there with me."

For the third time Megan shook her head. Only this time she let that be her only answer.

That and getting out of bed.

She kept the sheet around her and left Josh, going into the bathroom and closing the door behind her.

"Come on, Megan. You can't mean this," he called to her through that solid oak panel.

"I do mean it," she managed to answer the same way.

"And what am I supposed to do? Just put on my clothes and walk out of here? Pretend last night didn't happen and just say hi, how are you, when I pass you on the street?"

"Yes."

"No."

"Yes," she said, strongly enough to convey that she wasn't going to waver in her decision.

"You just want me to go?" he said in disbelief.

"Yes."

"Dammit, this is ridiculous."

"It's how I feel."

"Well, change how you feel."

The split-second right after that seemed to shout of the irony of that statement before she heard him sigh disgustedly and mutter, "Oh, geez," as if he knew he couldn't take it back or lessen the impact it had.

"Fine," he shouted in defeat. "If that's how you want it."

"That's how I want it," she barely whispered.

Megan listened intently to the sounds of Josh snatching up his clothes and storming out of her bedroom, out of her house, leaving behind him nothing but an empty, lonely silence.

Then she pressed the top of her head to the bathroom door and simply stood there, letting hot tears drop from her eyes onto her bare feet.

And as they did she couldn't help wondering how it had come to this, how it had come to this so quickly.

And what she'd done to screw up her karma so badly that she had to meet a man like Josh and still send him packing....

Chapter 12

WHAT HAD BEGUN AS A spectacular weekend on Friday night became one of the worst Megan had ever spent after the argument with Josh on Saturday morning. And that turned into a week that was not much better.

Business picked up remarkably, which would have been helpful in keeping her mind off the sheriff except that it seemed as if every second or third of her new clients named him as the person who had recommended acupuncture. Those clients frequently went on to talk about their own relationship with him—whether it be as a relative or a friend or just someone who had known him or his family forever.

It was interesting for Megan to see how right she'd been in believing that a high-profile client like the town sheriff could be a big boost to establishing her business with word-of-mouth recommendations, but each mention of Josh's name, each anecdote, just defeated what she was trying so hard to do—put him out of her thoughts.

Not that she was having much luck with that even when she didn't have a client bringing him into the conversation. It was as if he'd become for her what the latest cause became for her parents—an obsession. Because without a doubt, Josh was all Megan could think about.

Everything seemed to remind her of him. He was on her mind the minute she woke up in the morning. He was the last thing she thought about in bed at night. And many times in between she was so lost in the memory of him or something they'd done together or something he'd said, that she wasn't even aware of anything or anyone around her.

Which was exactly the case late on Friday afternoon as she stood in the break room with the teapot upturned over the sink, the tea long since having gone down the drain and Annissa saying her name in a way that let her know it hadn't been the first time her sister had called to her.

"Where is your head this week?" Nissa asked when Megan finally jolted back to reality.

"Sorry," Megan muttered as her sister turned off the hot plate she'd forgotten about.

Then Nissa took the teapot from her, set it on the counter, stretched out her arm to point her index finger at the love seat, and said, "Sit. Right now. And tell me what's going on."

Megan purposely *hadn't* told her sister what had happened with Josh when Nissa had returned from Denver Sunday night. She felt foolish. It didn't seem possible to have gotten in so deep with a man she'd basically just met and she hadn't wanted to admit it to her sister.

But now, as she did as she'd been told and sat on the

love seat, she decided that confiding in Nissa the way she usually did might help clear some of Josh out of her system. So she opted for being honest and open about it, letting Nissa know to just what extent she and Josh had gotten involved the previous week and what had happened on Saturday morning.

"And you think he's just a repeat of Noel?" Nissa asked when Megan was finished.

"Well, maybe not a repeat. But it seemed like there were a lot of similarities."

"Really? I wouldn't have thought so."

That surprised Megan. "Why not?"

"For one thing, you got Josh in here for acupuncture. You never could get Noel to try it. And now Josh must be telling people not only that he had it, but that it worked because so many of your appointments this week can be traced back to him. Noel wouldn't even tell anyone what you did for a living. Or let you tell them."

"True. But—"

"And for two, didn't you say when you met that couple on the street and you did your sex-of-the-baby prediction he just laughed about it? Can you imagine what Noel would have done? He'd have been mortified. He would have gone on and on about how he'd never be able to face those people again."

That was true, too.

"So what are you saying?" Megan asked defensively. "That I was wrong about Josh?"

"I don't know. Obviously, I didn't get to know him. But from what you've said about him he doesn't sound like a Noel-clone."

"So maybe I made a mountain out of a few mole-hills?" Megan muttered as it started to seem that way.

"Do you think that's what you did?"

"I think I better think about it."

The bell over the office door sounded to announce someone and Annissa glanced in that direction. "That'll be my four-thirty. Guess I'll leave you to your thinking. But do me a favor and don't turn on the hot plate. I swear you're going to burn us out with that thing and your wandering mind this week."

"Sorry," Megan repeated as her sister left the break room.

Being alone again was all it took for thoughts of Josh to spring back to life for Megan. Only now the thoughts were on a different track as she wondered if she really had taken a few minor things about him and built them into condemnable flaws.

Annissa was right about the acupuncture and about the sex-of-the-baby prediction. Josh's behavior on both counts was very different than Noel's.

Noel had had severe pollen allergies. But he'd popped numerous pills with just as numerous side effects all the while adamantly refusing to so much as consider giving acupuncture a try. Certainly he would never have touted the benefits of it to anyone else either; that would have required him letting it get out that acupuncture was actually what she did for a living.

And mortified was a good way to describe what Noel would have been in the same situation with the sex-of-the-baby prediction. Mortified. Embarrassed. Humiliated. Rattled.

But when Megan thought about it, she realized that Josh hadn't seemed to be any of those things. In fact, he'd joked about it and said he was going to hold her to the prediction. But she'd never had any indication that it was the big deal to him that it would have been to Noel.

And to be honest, she'd believed Josh when he'd explained that while he'd been embarrassed to be left at the altar by his former fiancée and to have to explain why to people, he hadn't been ashamed of the woman herself. Which was something else Megan couldn't say of Noel.

No, she hadn't thought of Noel as ashamed of her until Josh had pointed it out, but once he had she'd known that that was precisely what Noel had been—ashamed of her clothes, of her hair, of her jewelry, of her family, of her job. Ashamed of her. Which was why he'd wanted so badly to change her.

And that was the bigger issue, wasn't it? A man wanting to change her.

But had she made more of that with Josh than was actually there?

Meat in the refrigerator and a chair in front of the television?

Okay, yes, alone those were small things. But—

But what? she asked herself as if she were in an argument with someone else. There were no buts about it, meat in the refrigerator and a chair in front of the TV were definitely small things.

But at the time she'd felt as if those small things were just harbingers of bigger things to come.

Only now that she thought about them with some perspective, she had to admit that he hadn't been asking for any changes in her personally, just in some accommodations for him.

Compromises—that's what he'd said he was suggesting and now that she reconsidered, that's *all* she thought he was suggesting. But she'd taken it a step further on her own and decided he was asking her to make the kind of sacrifices Noel had wanted of her.

So maybe that initial panic she'd felt Saturday when Josh had begun to talk about wanting to be with her every night, every morning, had colored what she'd heard from then on. Maybe that was more what she'd been reacting to than Josh himself or what he was actually proposing.

Because in truth, Josh himself was not the man Noel was. Yes, Josh was conservative and a little leery of things that were off the beaten track. But he wasn't intolerant. And wasn't that what was really important? Tolerance of what she believed in and not trying to change her?

It seemed like it was.

So why had she turned him away? she asked herself.

But she knew the answer. Fear. Plain old ordinary fear that he would hurt her again the way Noel had hurt her.

But did she really think she had anything to fear from Josh? she asked herself.

She didn't. Not when she actually thought about it.

And not only didn't she have anything to fear from

him, she missed him so much she was miserable. She was more unhappy even than she had been when she and Noel had split up.

And there was only one reason for that.

Because in the short time she'd been with Josh she'd fallen in love with him.

More in love with him than she'd ever been with Noel.

But what about Josh? Was that how he felt about her? Was that what he'd been alluding to when he'd talked about wanting them to be together?

What else could he have meant? Just that he liked her a lot?

Well, okay, maybe. But deep down she didn't believe that. She believed that he had the same feelings for her that she had for him and that she'd made it so hard on him on Saturday morning that he hadn't gotten around to saying it.

Or at least that's what she hoped.

But one way or the other she would never know unless she swallowed her pride and went to him. Unless she told him the truth about what an idiot she'd been and how she felt about him.

And if he didn't feel the same?

She'd be crushed.

But even the possibility of being crushed couldn't keep her from at least going to him, talking to him.

Because if she didn't go to him, if she didn't talk to him, then there wouldn't be any chance at all.

And as strong as her feelings for Josh were, they just had to have a chance….

* * *

Megan and Nissa had driven into town in Nissa's car so Megan opted for walking the few blocks from her office to the courthouse where she hoped to find Josh. But she walked it in a hurry, her heart beating triple-time the whole way and a sort of prayerful chant repeating itself in her mind for Josh please not to think she was as nutty as his former fiancée to have rejected him so out-of-hand….

When she got to his office there was no one at the reception counter or behind it at her secretary's desk. Megan hoped she hadn't missed him, that he hadn't already gone home for the day or out on police business. Now that she'd made up her mind, she wanted this hurdle over with.

So even though there was no sound coming from Josh's office and she couldn't see anything through the glazed glass in the upper half of the door, she went around the counter, passed Millie's desk and knocked.

"In," came the command from the inner sanctum and Megan's pulse picked up more speed still.

She took a breath, breathed it out, and opened the door.

Josh was inside, his hips propped against the front of his desk, his legs stretched out and crossed at his ankles, arms folded over his uniform-shirted chest.

But he wasn't alone. In the two visitor's chairs were men Megan knew had to be his brothers from the resemblance she couldn't help but notice when they turned to look at her.

"Megan?" Josh said, shock in his voice but no warmth she could discern.

"Megan?" one of his brothers repeated with a hint of alarm in his tone as both of the other men sat up straighter and stared openly at her.

"Millie wasn't out front so I didn't know you were busy," Megan said, feeling the beginning of that treacherous panic that had gotten her into trouble a week earlier as she faced three men, not one of them looking as if they were glad to see her.

"Did you come to stick more pins in him?" one of the brothers muttered sarcastically and without a trace of friendliness, clearly referring to sticking pins in Josh metaphorically and not in terms of acupuncture.

"Scott," Josh said as a warning. Then, in a more normal tone, he said to both brothers, "We're about done here, aren't we? I can see you guys later, at home."

"Sure," the not-Scott brother agreed readily, while Scott continued to glare at her.

The not-Scott brother stood and roughly nudged Scott with a poke in the arm to do the same.

"We'll see you at home," not-Scott said.

Megan wanted to crawl into a hole but since there weren't any available she stepped out of the doorway to let the two other Brimley men go past her.

And if she'd thought that Scott's scorn was unnerving, it was nowhere near as bad as when she was suddenly left alone with Josh, standing in the doorway once more, the recipient of navy-blue eyes staring at her from beneath a frown that was much darker and more suspicious now that his brothers were gone and he was finished playing buffer for her.

"Hi," she said, knowing it sounded silly but unable to think of any other way to begin.

Josh just inclined his handsome head in answer.

And it *was* a handsome head. So incredibly handsome that it struck her all over again just how great-looking he was and made her stomach do a sensual little somersault.

"Did you need something?" he asked then, all business.

"To talk."

"Okay," he said as if his agreement were conditional. "Do you want to come in to talk or do you want to talk from the door?"

Megan stepped into the office and closed the door behind her.

But that was as far as she went and Josh didn't ask her to come any farther, or to sit down. Instead he continued to study her from beneath that frown, waiting, she thought, for her to say her piece and unwilling to help her out in any way.

But she wasn't sure where to start.

"Don't play games with me, Megan," he said then, a force to be reckoned with.

"I didn't come to play games. I just…I'm not sure how to say what I came to say."

"Just say it."

"You scared me," she blurted out. "I mean, last Saturday morning, what you were saying sort of threw me for a loop and I think I misjudged you."

Josh didn't respond to that. He merely went on studying her. Waiting still.

Megan decided she'd come this far, she might as well go the rest of the way, but it would have been easier if Josh had seemed more receptive. As it was, the whole time she told him about what she'd realized about him, about herself, he remained stony-faced.

"I can't stop being who I am. I *won't* stop being who I am," she said in conclusion when she'd covered everything.

Well, *almost* everything. She hadn't told him how she felt about him because she was worried what his lack of reaction meant and didn't want to go too far out onto that limb.

"But if you think you can take me the way I am…" She let her voice dwindle off, waiting herself now.

Josh didn't jump right in the way she wished he would have. For another eternal moment he just went on watching her as if weighing what she'd said against something she couldn't imagine.

But when he finally did speak, his words were music to her ears.

"I love you, Megan," he said matter-of-factly. "Just the way you are. I never asked you to be anything else."

"I know. I know. What you were talking about Saturday morning were only compromises. They weren't what I took them for. I was just paranoid, I guess," she said even as her mind was ringing with the fact that he'd told her he loved her.

Then his body language opened up, too. He uncrossed

his arms and cupped his hands around the edge of the
desk on either side of his hips.

"So where do we go from here?" he asked, obviously
not wanting to tap into that paranoia again and so leaving things up to her.

"I don't know. That every-night, every-morning thing
sounds pretty good now."

"Does that mean you'll marry me or is marriage
asking too much and you just want to live together?"

Her heart actually felt as if it were soaring. "Marriage
isn't asking too much. If you're asking."

"I was asking last Saturday."

"And now that you've had a week to think about
it?"

Josh pushed off the edge of the desk and came to her,
taking her into his arms. "Now that I've had a week to
think about it I'm asking again. Will you marry me?"

"I will."

"Because…"

"Because I love you, too."

Apparently that had been the correct answer because
it made him smile for the first time since she'd shown
up there.

"You have put me through one lousy week," he com-
plained good-naturedly then.

"I take it that's why your brothers looked like they
wanted to string me up."

"They'll get over it."

"But I understand your allergy is better. Don't I get
points for that?"

"You cured my sneezing and broke my heart."

"Haven't I fixed that, too, now?" she said, tilting her chin to look up at his ruggedly handsome face.

"Mmm. Pretty much."

"Only pretty much?"

He kissed her, a long, lingering kiss, as if that was what he needed to mend his broken heart. But then, as if it hadn't been enough, he said, "I think I need a deeper balm."

"Oh? What did you have in mind?"

He showed her by pulling her so close she could feel the hard ridge of his desire for her.

"Here?" she asked with a scandalized laugh.

"I think it's what I need," he reiterated with mock sincerity. "Then I can be convinced that you're giving yourself to me, heart and soul."

"You're evil."

He grinned to prove it. "I guess you better get used to the idea of marrying an evil man."

"There's no lock on the door," Megan said with a glance over her shoulder in that direction.

"Millie's gone for the day."

"What if someone else comes in?"

"If they come in without knocking they deserve what they get."

"And here I thought you were conservative," she said as he kissed a path down the side of her neck to the hollow of her throat and lit tiny sparks in her bloodstream.

"Maybe it's you who's changin' me."

"I don't want you changed. I want you just the way you are, too."

"And I want you on that couch."

Which was just where he took her, to the overstuffed sofa that lined the wall opposite his desk, capturing her mouth again as he laid them both down, his body more on top of hers than not.

But Megan didn't protest. The sense of wickedness that went with doing something completely inappropriate in his office just added to the titillation.

Not that she needed any more than she was getting as Josh unfastened the buttons that held her smock dress closed down the front and unclasped her front-hook bra, too. Certainly she didn't need more titillation than she was getting when his hand closed over her already engorged breast and began to work his wonders with her nipple.

But if she was going to be exposed she decided he was, too, and she didn't hesitate to pull his shirttails from his jeans, to undo his buttons and slip the uniform shirt off his shoulders so she could have access to his glorious back and shoulders and biceps and pectorals.

By then the week-long hunger for him that Megan had been fighting grew bigger than she was and she lost all awareness of where they were, of everything but Josh and being there with him, having him do all the things she'd lain in her bed and torturously relived each night since last Friday.

But this was no torture as somewhere along the way his jeans came off and she came all the way out of her dress and her underthings. As his mouth and tongue and hands explored her, aroused her, nearly drove her wild. As she filled her own hands, her own mouth, her own senses with every inch of him until neither of them could stand not to be joined and he slipped into her as seamlessly as if he were meant to be a part of her.

And together they rode the tidal wave of a passion set free. A passion they now could—and did—indulge in without inhibition. A passion that sealed them as one and gifted them with an ecstatic peak of pleasure so intense neither of them could do anything but hold on to the other and let it take them higher and higher, melding their bodies, their spirits, their lives into one.

And when that passion, that ecstasy, had spent itself, they settled in the soft cushions of the couch, Josh on his side, the wonderfully heavy weight of his thigh across hers, as he kissed her again. A deep, replete, bonding kiss.

"I do love you, Megan," he whispered.

"Weirdnesses and all?"

"Weirdnesses and all."

"Good. Because I love you, too."

"Conservativeness and all?"

She glanced down at their naked, entwined bodies. "Oh yeah, conservativeness and all," she said with a laugh.

"Besides, maybe you aren't so weird," Josh added. "I met Kate McDermot today and she told me to tell you she had an ultrasound and you were right—she's having a girl."

"Of course I was right," Megan said. But that wasn't the only thing she felt confident about. As Josh kissed her once more, sweetly, slowly, and with passion rising between them again already, Megan also felt confident that despite their differences they really could have a future together as man and wife.

Because in that moment when his mouth was plundering hers yet again, when his hands began the miracles they could work on her body, and his desire for her was making itself known, she knew without a doubt that none of their differences were greater than the love they shared.

The love they would go on sharing for the rest of their lives.

The love that would allow them to celebrate their differences, to revel in them, and to accept each other without ever asking for more.

* * * * *

Fall in Love with...

MEN
in UNIFORM

MUBPA10

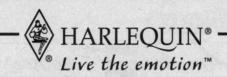

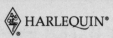

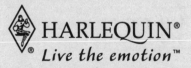

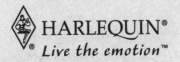

HARLEQUIN®
Presents®

The world's bestselling romance series...
The series that brings you your favorite authors,
month after month:

Helen Bianchin...Emma Darcy
Lynne Graham...Penny Jordan
Miranda Lee...Sandra Marton
Anne Mather...Carole Mortimer
Melanie Milburne...Michelle Reid

and many more talented authors!

Wealthy, powerful, gorgeous men...
Women who have feelings just like your own...
The stories you love, set in exotic, glamorous locations...

HARLEQUIN®
Presents®

Seduction and Passion Guaranteed!

HPDIR08

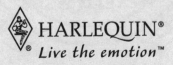

Harlequin® Historical
Historical Romantic Adventure!

Imagine a time of chivalrous knights and unconventional ladies, roguish rakes and impetuous heiresses, rugged cowboys and spirited frontierswomen— these rich and vivid tales will capture your imagination!

Harlequin Historical . . . they're too good to miss!